"What do you think about m̲

"That's a loaded question," Alec said.

"Is it?" Scarlet asked.

"Si," he said.

This close she couldn't help but notice the light stubble and firm, full lips that she knew felt just right pressed against her.

Scarlet felt a jolt of desire go through her and blinked, taking a step back. She hadn't come here to hook up again—but she'd never been one to walk away from something she wanted.

And she wanted Alec Velasquez.

She put her hand on his chest, running her finger against the skin exposed by the buttons he'd left undone at his collar.

"Tell me what you're thinking, Alejandro," she said softly, hearing the lust in her own voice.

Without breaking eye contact, he brought his mouth closer to hers.

"I'm thinking that if I don't kiss you, I think I might die," he admitted. Then his mouth brushed over hers, and his hand tangled in her hair.

This was what she'd been waiting for...and it was worth the wait.

* * *

One Night, Two Secrets is a part
of the One Night series.

Dear Reader,

I hope you enjoyed *One Night with His Ex* last month! I had so much fun writing Mauricio and Hadley's story and really enjoyed introducing Alec at the end to add some drama. I have a friend who always says that no good deed goes unpunished, and that's what happened with Alec standing in for his brother. He meant well, but it has completely spiraled out of his control.

He likes Scarlet and wants to get in touch with her, but how would that conversation go? "Oh, hey, remember me? I pretty much lied about everything, but I like you and want to get to know you better!" That's where this story opens. Two secrets—one his and one hers. And those secrets make it hard for them to trust each other.

I think that most of us don't start out trying to deceive or hurt someone by keeping secrets, but there comes a point when the secret takes over your life. My dad—the smartest man I know—always says that once you start lying you have to keep lying. There's no way back to the truth. In real life, as well as in fiction, this is so true.

Happy reading,

Katherine Garbera

KATHERINE GARBERA

———

ONE NIGHT, TWO SECRETS

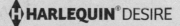

Recycling programs
for this product may
not exist in your area.

ISBN-13: 978-1-335-60402-6

One Night, Two Secrets

Printed in U.S.A.

Katherine Garbera is the *USA TODAY* bestselling author of more than ninety-five books. Her writing is known for its emotional punch and sizzling sensuality. She lives in the Midlands of the UK with the love of her life; her son, who recently graduated university; and a spoiled miniature dachshund. You can find her online on at www.katherinegarbera.com and on Facebook, Twitter and Instagram.

Books by Katherine Garbera

Harlequin Desire

The Wild Caruthers Bachelors

Tycoon Cowboy's Baby Surprise
The Tycoon's Fiancée Deal
Craving His Best Friend's Ex

Cole's Hill Bachelors

Rancher Untamed

One Night

One Night with His Ex
One Night, Two Secrets

Visit her Author Profile page at Harlequin.com, or katherinegarbera.com, for more titles.

You can find Katherine Garbera on Facebook, along with other Harlequin Desire authors, at Facebook.com/harlequindesireauthors.

This book is dedicated to my kids, Courtney and Lucas. I'm so proud of the adults you've become. You know I love you more than words and that you both mean the world to me. Someday I'll have to reveal that my favorite child is... Just kidding! I couldn't choose between the both of you.

One

Throwing up three mornings in a row wasn't unheard-of for an O'Malley. After all, they were a family known to live life to the fullest, and that often involved excess. But Scarlet hadn't been drinking for weeks, ever since her best friend, Siobahn Murphy, lead singer for the hottest girl group since Destiny's Child, had broken up with her fiancé and he'd immediately eloped to Vegas with Siobahn's main rival. The paparazzi had been on Siobahn 24/7, and Scarlet had wanted to keep her wits about her to help protect her friend. She'd had her own experiences being hounded by the press, and wouldn't wish it on anyone.

Now Siobahn was safely ensconced in the guest room of Scarlet's East Hampton cottage, being watched over by Billie, Scarlet's personal assistant.

As Scarlet splashed water on her face, she went through all the reasons she might be throwing up. Food poisoning wasn't the issue. No one else staying here had been sick and her personal chef, Lourdes, was pretty scrupulous about kitchen hygiene.

"Not food poisoning," she muttered aloud as she wiped her face with a muslin cloth recommended by her aesthetician. At twenty-eight, she didn't have many fine lines or signs of aging, but still, her mother had always said it was never too late to take steps to prevent them.

You're distracting yourself from the obvious.

Scarlet looked in the mirror, knowing the voice was in her mind and that she was alone. She'd lost her sister three years ago to a drug overdose, but that hadn't stopped Scarlet from still hearing her voice at odd moments. Usually when she least wanted to hear it.

Tara had been a bossy older sister and apparently didn't want to stop giving her orders. Scarlet sighed and stared down at her stomach. She hadn't had a period in over six weeks even though she'd always been regular as clockwork.

Yup, you're preggers. Wish I was still there to see the old man's face when he hears the news.

"Shut up, Tay. I'm not even sure yet." Scarlet

couldn't believe she was talking to herself, and that she was even in this situation to begin with.

If there was one thing the O'Malleys were good at, it was making money, living life full on and making colossally bad decisions. It went all the way back to her mother, who'd died when Scarlet was seventeen. Dying under mysterious circumstances that had been concluded an accident but many believed might have been more deliberate. Her father was on his sixth wife, and that didn't count the mistresses he'd had in between and often during those liaisons. Scarlet's longest relationship to date was twelve days, and honestly, she knew that was because they'd been on her private island and Leon's private plane couldn't land because of high winds.

She couldn't be pregnant.

If she was…

God, this was a nightmare.

She knew the responsible thing would be to give the child up. Everyone said she was spoiled, and she took it as a compliment. Her goal had always been to live her best life.

But a kid?

She had a few acquaintances who had children but they tended to employ an army of nannies to care for them. Her own childhood had shown her how alienating that could be.

She walked into her bedroom and fell back on her bed, staring up at the ceiling that she'd had painted to resemble the night sky. As she looked up at the "stars," Lulu, her miniature dachshund, bounded up the ramp that Scarlet kept next to the bed and hopped on her stomach. She petted her sweet little dog as she lay there trying to ignore the inevitable.

What about the dad?

Tara's voice again.

The dad?

That's right… Mauricio Velasquez. *Texan Humanitarian of the Year.* Other than drinking too much with her and hooking up for one night, he was pretty rock solid. And he'd told her about his large family and how close they all were.

She put her hand on her stomach again. Mauricio might be the best chance this baby had…if there was one. She'd have Billie get Dr. Patel to drop by later on today. If she was pregnant, she'd book a trip for herself, Billie and Siobahn to Cole's Hill. The tiny town might be the perfect place for Siobahn to recover from her breakup while Scarlet checked out her baby daddy.

Four hours later she was sitting on the couch across from Billie and Siobahn, who were both staring at her as if she'd lost her ever-loving mind. To be fair, she might have.

"Texas?" Siobahn asked again. "No way. That's the last place I want to be chased by paparazzi."

"Precisely my point," Scarlet reminded her friend. "They won't follow you there. It's the perfect move.

I rented a house this morning in something called the Five Families neighborhood, which has a manned security gate. We'll have plenty of privacy."

"But why Texas?" Billie asked. "I mean, I don't mind going, but it's hot in Texas in July."

Not as hot as it was going to be when she found Mauricio Velasquez. Dang, but the two of them had burned up the sheets during their one night together.

"I need to see someone there, and we could all use a break," Scarlet said. "Trust me. It will be fun, and Siobahn, you'll forget all about Maté."

"I already have," her friend said.

"Liar," Scarlet said in a kind tone. She walked over and sat down on the arm of Siobahn's chair and hugged her friend.

"This will be good for both of us," Scarlet promised.

Siobahn looked up at her, and it broke Scarlet's heart to see her usually bubbly friend's sad, red-rimmed eyes. She would do whatever it took to distract Siobahn, and though she hadn't mentioned it to her friend, Scarlet knew that this pregnancy was going to be a distraction for both of them.

Dr. Patel had confirmed it—she was going to have a child. Scarlet was still reeling from the news but she'd always been the kind of girl who dealt with things by getting busy and moving. She couldn't stay in New York City or the Hamptons. She had to see

Mauricio again and then she'd figure out this entire baby thing.

If there was one thing the O'Malleys were bad at it was taking care of someone else.

A baby.

She had always wanted someone of her own to love, but she had promised herself that she'd never have kids. She'd seen firsthand what happened when the wrong sort of people had kids. And she had never been anyone's idea of a "good girl."

She put her hand on her stomach and looked in the mirror. Mauricio Velasquez was a decent guy. He'd won a humanitarian award. He'd be a good father, right?

She'd meet his family and make sure, but she wanted everything for this baby that she'd never had. Two loving parents, and a family support network so that her baby wouldn't turn out like her.

Sunday brunch with the parents was a Velasquez tradition, one that Alec Velasquez had been lucky enough to miss for the last month thanks to various speaking engagements at different technology symposia around the globe. In fact, if he could figure out a way to miss this week, he would do it, as well.

He hadn't been back to Cole's Hill since the fiasco where he'd posed as his twin brother, Mauricio, to accept a humanitarian award on Mo's behalf in Houston and—damn. He'd had the night of his life with Scarlet O'Malley. But there'd been no way for him to contact her again. He'd tried to come up with a plan where he'd go to New York and just casually run into her, but then he kept coming up against how to tell her he wasn't Mo. He knew straight off that no woman liked being lied to like that.

At least he'd spoken on the phone to Mo's girlfriend, Hadley Everton, and cleared things up with her. After initially thinking it was Mo in the tabloid photos with Scarlet from that night, Hadley had been able to sort it out with him. And now they were engaged. That made their mom so happy she'd almost been okay with Alec missing all those brunches.

But she knew he was back in town and she wanted answers. Given that Hadley and Mo were engaged, everyone knew it was Alec who had hooked up with Scarlet O'Malley. Around town, the gossips referred to her as "the heiress." And unless he wanted to deal with the full force of his mother's temper, he'd be at brunch.

He sat down at his laptop and looked at the email to Scarlet he'd saved in his drafts folder. He kept changing it but every time he read it he knew he couldn't send it to her. He should be happy they had one night together and let it go.

He heard the ding of his security system and suspected it might be his twin brother, who had texted him that they could ride together out to the polo grounds where brunch was being held today.

He hid the email window on his computer and stood up just as his brother entered the room. The walls of Alec's home office were lined with leather-bound volumes of books; the interior designer had thought they would make the study look more elegant. But Alec had insisted that the books all be ones he'd read. So there was an entire shelf of Goosebumps and Harry Potter, all leather-bound, right below the Shakespeare and Hemingway.

"Morning, bro."

"Morning," Alec said. They did the one-arm bro hug and then he stepped back. "Where is your better half?"

"There was some sort of emergency with Helena's wedding and she had to go see Kinley this morning to solve it," Mo said. Hadley's sister, Helena, was planning a wedding to her high school sweetheart, Malcolm. They had faced a rough patch recently when Mal had gambled away their wedding fund. But the couple had come back together stronger than ever.

Kinley Quinten-Caruthers was a sought after wedding planner working for the famous Jaqs Veerland. Kinley was a hometown girl who'd moved back to Cole's Hill a few years ago to open a Texas branch to service high profile clients including former NFL bad boy Hunter Caruthers, who became her brother-in-law after she married Nathan Caruthers, the father of her child.

"What kind of emergency? It's a Sunday."

Mauricio shrugged and shook his head. "I have no idea. I'm told it's better not to know."

"Indeed," Alec said. "I guess we should be heading out."

"Before we do…"

"I knew it."

"Knew what?"

"That you were here for something other than to carpool," Alec said.

"Well, you've been shifty recently."

"Shifty?" Alec asked, arching one eyebrow.

"Mom's words. She suggested I use our twin connection to find out what's going on with you," Mo said, pacing over to the bookshelf. "I didn't want to tell her that it's probably a girl problem because that would activate her matrimony radar and you'd never have a moment's peace today."

"Thanks for that."

"You need to come up with something I can tell her," Mo said.

"Yeah, we don't want a replay of what happened when we were kids and you told Mom that I skipped soccer practice to talk to a girl." Alec smiled at the memory.

Harking back to their childhood provided a momentary distraction, but he knew that Mo wasn't going to let this go that easily. While neither of them believed in a psychic twin sense, they'd always been able to perceive when the other brother was in turmoil.

"And still it's a woman causing you problems—wanna talk about it? We have some time before we are due at the polo grounds."

Did he want to talk about it? Hell, no. He wasn't a touchy-feely sort of guy, and to be fair, neither was Mo.

"Not really."

"Okay."

"Okay? Mom would be so disappointed," Alec said.

"No she wouldn't. I suspect that Bianca is going to be the next one to try to figure out what's going on with you."

Alec groaned. Their sister would be a lot more persistent. Even though she was a year younger than the two of them, she'd always had a way of getting what she wanted from all of the Velasquez men.

"I don't think there's anything that can be done about this," Alec said. "It's Scarlet. I can't stop thinking about her but I can't contact her because she thinks I'm you. If I say, 'Hey, I was pretending to be my brother,' I don't think she's going to want to see me again."

There, he'd said it. And saying it out loud made him realize how ridiculous the entire thing was. He and Mo were thirty years old, almost thirty-one. The time for switching places with his twin had long passed.

Mo clapped Alec's shoulder.

"That is a tough one. But if I learned anything from my relationship with Hadley, it's that if you want a woman badly enough, you go after her. Apologize for your mistakes, tell her the truth and then tell her how you feel."

"Ugh. That's a lot of telling."

"Maybe you could write an app that would do it for you," Mo said sarcastically.

"Screw you."

But Alec felt better after talking to Mo. Maybe he would call Scarlet or even take the jet to New York and see her. It wouldn't hurt. And then he'd have an idea if this obsession was simply because she was out of reach or if it was something else.

When they finally arrived in Cole's Hill, Siobahn decided to stay at the house but Scarlet was eager to find Mauricio right away and talk to him about the pregnancy. She had Lulu in the large bag that she carried her in when they were in a new place and Billie by her side as they drove into town for coffee.

She wasn't sure what kind of man he was; after all they'd spent only one night together and they'd both been drinking and dancing and laughing. When she'd woken up the next morning, he'd been gone, and she didn't blame him after she'd seen the paparazzi pictures from the night before that had ended up on TMZ.

Her life wasn't for everyone, but she'd gotten used to it. Tara used to say they'd been born a goldfish bowl and like good little guppies they'd learned how to preen for the press. There were times when Scarlet wished for a simpler, less public life, but to be honest she loved it most days.

In this town, though, no one seemed to pay her the least bit of attention. She could get used to this. When she stopped into the coffee shop to get her coconut milk latte, everyone left her alone.

"Do you know the Velasquez family?" Scarlet causally asked the barista after ordering.

"Everyone knows them. They're legends in Cole's Hill. I think they'll all be out at the new polo grounds today. I don't follow the sport but there's a former professional scheduled to play today... Dee, do you remember his name?" the barista asked the woman at the espresso machine.

"Bartolome Figueras. He's also a model. Oh, my, he's good-looking," Dee said.

"He is," Scarlet agreed. She had met him and his sister at a polo match in Bridgehampton earlier in the summer. She might even have his number. "I love polo. Do you think that we could attend the match?" Scarlet said, turning to Billie, who smiled.

"I'm sure you could. They've been doing monthly matches to raise money for a housing charity that

Mauricio Velasquez runs," the barista said. She pushed a button on her register and some receipt paper came out. She ripped it off and jotted down a website.

"I think you can get all of the information from here," she said, handing the paper to Scarlet. "Have fun."

When they had their orders, Scarlet and Billie walked out of the coffee shop toward the parking lot.

"That was surprisingly easy," Billie said.

"It was. Let's go home and get changed. I bet Siobahn will want to join us," Scarlet said.

"I don't know about that. She's sort of in a funk this morning."

Scarlet stopped walking and turned to her assistant. Billie had been picking up the slack the last few days, looking after Siobahn for her while Scarlet had been trying to figure out this pregnancy thing. She hadn't mentioned the test results to anyone, even Billie. Only she and Dr. Patel knew.

"I should have stopped in to see her. I'm sorry I've been so focused on finding Mauricio."

"It's okay. I'm just saying I don't know if you're going to be able to persuade her to come with you to the polo match."

"Fair enough," Scarlet said.

They went back to the house. While Billie tracked down contact info for Bartolome Figueras's assistant and texted her to put their names on the VIP list, Scarlet talked with Siobahn. She wasn't in the mood to leave the house, so Scarlet left Lulu with her.

The polo grounds were busy when they arrived. Billie went to see if she could find out where the stables were. Scarlet moved through the crowds, searching the men who were dressed in traditional polo shirts and jodhpurs, scanning for the one she'd spent the night with.

She saw Bart first, and heard his sister Zaria's laughter. Scarlet smiled at the sound of it. The Argentinean heiress had a big, bold laugh that matched her personality. Scarlet headed toward them, then noticed Mauricio Velasquez was standing in the same group. He had his arm around a very pretty woman with thick dark curly hair that hung to the middle of her back. She watched them for a minute. Maybe she was his sister. But then he bent to kiss the woman, and not in a sisterly way.

Scarlet had never in her life been a timid person, and seeing the father of her unborn child kiss another woman made her angry. For a split second she realized she'd had a little fantasy of some sort of perfect rendezvous where they'd instantly agree to spend the rest of their lives together.

It was as if she'd forgotten she was an O'Malley and that kind of thing wasn't in the cards for her. She didn't do commitment. She wasn't programmed for long term. She'd seen what that had done to her mother, who couldn't handle being left by Scarlet's father as he'd moved on to someone younger, hotter and a little bit wilder.

Tara had been the same as their father, living fast and hard and burning bright for such a short time. But Scarlet had been confused, caught between two opposites. On the one hand, she had the dream of having the perfect family that at times she saw in old pictures of the O'Malleys taken when she was a child. And then there was the reality that she had never been responsible for anyone but herself.

O'Malleys were better when they only had to look out for themselves. It was what they were the best at…that and doing something outrageous and creating scandal.

Plastering a smile on her face, she strode determinedly toward the group, forcing herself not to look at the woman or Mauricio again. Instead she'd just play it cool and pretend she was here to see Bart. But as she got closer, she couldn't prevent her gaze from straying to Mauricio.

He was still handsome—damn him. For a brief second she wondered if there was a world where the Velasquez good would balance out her O'Malley bad. She'd heard nothing but good things about the Velasquez family and how close knit they were.

And it had created a longing inside her for the family that she'd never had and had always been a little curious about. Even though she wasn't built for commitment, it might be nice to be a part of this kind of thing for real.

"Scarlet," Bart said in his wonderfully accented English. "What a surprise! I'm glad you're here. Please meet my friends Mauricio Velasquez and his fiancée, Hadley Everton."

Fiancée?

What the hell?

She turned toward the man she thought she knew and noticed the set of his shoulders and the scar on his eyebrow. The man she'd slept with didn't have that. What the hell was going on?

"Hello, Mauricio," she said. "I believe we've met. At that gala in Houston."

"Well, actually—" Mauricio began.

"I'm the one you're looking for," a male voice said from behind her.

She turned to face the man and was struck speechless. He was a mirror image of Mauricio. He had a twin? In that moment, Scarlet realized that in true O'Malley fashion this situation had gone from bad to worse. A baby scare from a one-night stand? Sure, it happened. But learning that her baby daddy was an impostor, a virtual stranger whom she knew nothing about... Well, that was the old O'Malley bad luck.

Two

Alec really wished he'd figured out a way to send that email. The look on Scarlet's face as she turned to face him was one of shock, followed quickly by disdain and anger. He'd actually never had a woman look at him like that before and he didn't like it.

He prided himself on being a good guy.

He had always treated women with respect—he had a sister after all. He never wanted to be the kind of man who did anything to incur this kind of look.

In his head words swirled around like computer code when he was trying to figure out a new algorithm. He sorted through them with lightning speed.

But this wasn't the time to really talk. Bart, Mo,

Hadley and the others were all staring at him. Mo and Hadley at least knew what was going on, but to everyone else… It had to seem crazy.

He reached for Scarlet's arm, to draw her away and speak privately, trying to ignore the fact that her honey-blond hair, falling in waves to her shoulders, seemed even thicker and more tempting than he remembered. Her gray-green eyes sparkled with temper as she shrugged away from his arm and turned, the full skirt of her flowy dress swinging around her legs. Her shoulders were straight as she headed toward a copse of trees on the edge of the polo grounds. Alec had no choice but to follow her.

She stumbled on the grass and he reached out to steady her.

"Thanks."

He nodded. He couldn't believe she was here. Or that his lie had been found out in such a public way. He knew he'd screwed up.

When they finally reached the shade of the trees, he immediately launched into an apology. "I'm sorry. I should have told you everything that night. Mauricio was sick with food poisoning and he asked me to step in and accept the award for him. For some reason, I thought it would just be easier to let everyone think I was Mauricio, instead of having to explain his absence. I didn't want the organizers to think that Mo had blown them off. It goes back to how we handled things like this when we were young. I should have told you, too, but by the time I realized my mistake, it was too late," he said.

She tipped her head back, lifting the hat that he hadn't realized she was carrying in one of her hands and settling it over her hair. Then she drew out a pair of large dark sunglasses and put them on.

"I don't accept your apology," she said. "Who are you? I don't even know your name."

Shame made him shake his head. How could he ever make this up to her? "I'm Alejandro. Mauricio and I are twins. My friends call me Alec."

"That's good to know, Alejandro. I think you should have told me when we got back to my hotel room."

"We were too busy with…other things to talk at that point," he said in his defense. "But you're right. I definitely should have stopped and told you who I was. I meant to do it in the morning but by then our photo was going viral and I knew my brother was going to be in hot water with Hadley. And I rushed out to try to warn him. Not that you should take that as an excuse."

She crossed her arms under her breasts and his gaze drifted down for a moment. He enjoyed the deep V of the bodice of her wrap dress before he realized what he was doing and brought his eyes back up to meet hers.

"Fair enough. I get why you left," she said.

"I'm sorry," he said. Was it actually that easy? He'd been afraid to let her know and now it seemed his worry had been for nothing. He might actually be able to ask her out and maybe get something started.

She nodded. "Actually, I need to talk to you about that night."

Talking was good. *Right?* He was a practical man. A rational man. But he'd been raised by parents who believed in fate and destiny, and a part of him thought Scarlet's presence in Cole's Hill had to be more than just coincidence. But what was it?

He easily attributed his longing for her to the fact that one night hadn't been enough for him. It never was. One weekend…maybe. But one night—no way! Now he was standing in front of her and that ache he'd felt when he'd been trying not to think about her for the last six weeks was stronger than ever. So he wasn't going to walk away from it.

He'd learned early on that the more he denied he wanted something, the more he craved it. But Scarlet hardly seemed like she was going to give him a second chance.

And really, did he blame her?

No, of course not.

His smart watch buzzed, warning him he needed to head to the barn to get ready for the polo match.

He scrubbed his hand over his face and wished for once that he had more self-control. Though following his gut had led him to great success in business, this wasn't the first time it had landed him in hot water with his personal life.

"I have about ten minutes before the match starts," Alec said. "My family is having a brunch afterward and I'd love it if you would accompany me. So you can see I'm not a total douchebag."

"I don't think you're a *total* douchebag."

He almost smiled at the way she said it but he knew he was still in hot water. It reminded him of why he'd hooked up with her. She'd been so spot-on with her descriptions of some of the more pretentious people in the room the night of the awards banquet, they'd sort of started bonding over it.

"Will you please come with me?" he asked. "They all know what I did…well, at least that I kissed you while pretending to be Mo. So they will definitely understand you're angry with me."

"My assistant is here. Can she come, too?"

"Yes, of course. I think Bart and Zaria will be joining us, too, so there will be more familiar faces for you."

"Fine. I'll see you after the match," she said, walking past him in a cloud of feminine ire and Chanel perfume. He glanced over his shoulder, watching her retreat and ignoring the spark of excitement that was spreading through him.

She kept her cool until she was sure she was out of his line of sight and then she finally stopped walking like she had all the confidence in the world.

Whom the hell had she slept with?

She'd made some dumb decisions in the course of her life. Heck, who hadn't, right? But the truth was she was usually pretty picky when it came to bed partners. She didn't hook up with just every cute guy who came along, despite what the tabloids liked to print about her. And that night… Well, she'd thought she was connecting with Mauricio Velasquez. As for Alejandro—Alec—she'd had no idea she was being tricked like that.

Ugh.

"You okay?" Billie asked, coming up next to her.

"Yeah. I mean no. I don't know," she admitted to her assistant. "This isn't going like I planned."

Billie laughed in that honest way of hers and Scarlet couldn't help smiling. "When does it ever? What's going on here? You haven't told me a single deet except you wanted to reconnect with that guy you met in Houston."

Scarlet took her sunglasses off and glanced at her friend, trying to find the words. But they still escaped her. This was the kind of situation Tara had always found herself in. Usually Scarlet prided herself on being smarter about her personal life.

"It's complicated," she said.

"I'm all ears," Billie said.

"Well, I can't say too much here," Scarlet said, glancing around at all the people gathering on the observation deck to watch the match. There was a bar set up and a small buffet table. The conversation was about the Velasquez brothers; apparently one of them was married to the British jewelry heiress Phillipa Hamilton-Hoff.

"Later, then?" Billie asked.

Scarlet nodded.

"Do you need me? I thought I'd go back to the house and check on Siobahn and then go grocery shopping. I have two interviews lined up for later this evening with private chefs but I'm probably going to have to cook dinner tonight," Billie said.

Billie was obviously busy, and a part of Scarlet knew she should just let her get on with her job. What was she going to say to Billie?

"Scar?"

She just shrugged and shoved her glasses back on her face and turned away. The quick movement made her stomach churn.

Crap.

She didn't want to throw up here. She couldn't.

But she felt the bile in the back of her throat and put her hand in front of her mouth.

"Bathroom?" she said to Billie.

"Shit. Too far," Billie said, quickly realizing that Scarlet was going to throw up. Billie grabbed her hand and they started running away from the crowd as the first chukka of the polo match got under way. Billie drew her behind the side of the barn in the nick of time and Scarlet was sick while Billie squeezed her shoulder and held her hair out of the way.

When her stomach was empty, Billie handed her a water bottle and she rinsed her mouth and spit before standing up and turning to her friend. She'd lost her sunglasses somewhere and she needed them.

She liked the illusion that she was invisible hiding behind the large-framed glasses. And as she saw the surprised look Billie's brown eyes, she knew she needed to hide. Her friend wasn't going to buy any excuse. She knew for a fact that Scarlet had been on a detox, eating and drinking healthy.

"You're pregnant?"

Scarlet swallowed, her throat dry and sore. "Yes. But it's complicated."

"The father is that Mauricio guy?" Billie asked, taking a few steps away from Scarlet and picking up her sunglasses from the ground.

She handed them to Scarlet and she put them on. "I thought so. But the guy has a twin brother. They switched places that night."

"Okay, obviously we are mad about this. What do you want me to do? I can reach out to our press contacts and start a smear—"

"Not yet. I don't even know this guy. He invited me to join him and his family for brunch after the match. I was hoping you'd come with me," Scarlet said.

"Oh, hell yes, I'll be there. What's his name?" Billie asked, pulling her smartphone from her pocket.

"Alejandro Velasquez," Scarlet said.

"Shit, are you kidding?"

"Do you think I'd joke about that? Why? Who is he?"

"Well, let me do a quick internet search to confirm it but I'm pretty sure he's a tech genius who owns a billion-dollar software company."

"So why would he do something so immature, like pretending to be his brother?" Scarlet asked. "B, what am I going to do? You know my family… I thought—"

"I'll do some research while you watch the match. Then at this brunch thing we can see what kind of family he has, what kind of people they are. Maybe the switching-places thing was innocent. Whatever happens you've got me by your side," Billie said as she hugged Scarlet.

She wasn't alone. Why, then, did she always feel that way? Billie was the best assistant she'd ever had but, in a way, she was just like the nanny Scarlet and Tara had shared growing up. Paid family. Though she knew Billie wasn't with her just for a paycheck.

"Thanks, B," she said. "This has completely screwed with my head."

"That's saying something. Nothing ever rattles you."

She had to smile at that. She had built up a resistance to the kinds of situations that would freak out most people. But this… Maybe it was the fact that Tara wasn't here for her to talk to about it. Tara would be able to make her laugh about it even though a part of her was hurt.

Scarlet couldn't help but think that maybe he hadn't worried about lying to her because of who she was. Because she was the kind of person who'd lived her life going from one scandal to the next. She had a reputation. So lying to her hadn't worried him.

She hoped that wasn't the case.

But then she'd learned that hoping was a waste of time. She'd hoped her dad would stop marrying younger women and actually be a parent to her and Tara. She'd hoped that Tara would stop using and get clean. Now she was hoping that Alejandro Velasquez was a decent guy…

Alec had grown up playing polo with his brothers. The Velasquez family had been horse breeders for generations, and Alec's dad had been playing on a team with Tio Jose and their cousins since they were children. So riding was second nature to Alec. His four-player team generally consisted of Alec, Mo, their eldest brother, Diego, and the youngest Velasquez, Inigo, with either Malcolm Ferris—Mo's best friend—or their dad often subbing for Inigo, who was gone a lot of the time on the Formula 1 circuit. Technically Inigo wasn't supposed to play when he was home because of insurance concerns, but the Velasquez men had a problem with following the rules.

Diego was always number one—the goal striker.

He'd always had a good eye for hitting goals, so it made sense for him to play in that position. Alec and Mauricio traded off being number two, the forward, and number three, the pivotal player who switches between offense and defense. Then number four protected the goal. Malcolm was really good at that position and since they'd grown up playing with him, he knew everyone's strengths and weaknesses.

But when the third chukka ended, Alec knew his brothers and Malcolm weren't pleased with his performance. It didn't help that they were playing against Bart and his friends, who'd all played polo professionally at some point in their lives.

Alec hung back from the others trying to search out Scarlet in the crowd. He finally spotted her standing with Zaria and laughing at something Bart's sister had said. Scarlet's head was thrown back and he felt a jolt of lust just seeing her happiness.

"You're not going to be in a state to even talk to her if you don't get your head in the game," Mo said, coming over to him.

His twin was known for his hot temper, but since he and Hadley had gotten engaged, Mauricio hadn't been giving in to it as often. For a while after Hadley and Mo had broken up he'd been getting into fights with everyone in town and drinking way too much. It had been Mo's way of dealing with losing Hadley while not having to admit he'd pushed her away.

"I'm trying," Alec said. "I wasn't expecting to see

her today. Why is she here? And how am I going to make up for lying about being you?" he asked his twin. She'd thrown him and he wasn't used to being caught off guard. Part of the reason he was so successful was that he could usually envision all the possibilities in a situation. But this was completely out of left field. He'd done some research on Scarlet—she was known for moving forward and rarely going back to anything or anyone.

Mo sighed. "Dude, I have no clue but winning the game would probably go a long way to impressing her."

Alec knew the outcome of this match didn't matter to her at all. "I think that would make you happy, not her."

"Maybe your right… But damn, you're in trouble now."

"What?" he asked, glancing over at Scarlet and noticing that his sister, who was almost six months pregnant, and his mom had joined the group Scarlet was in.

Oh crap. That was all he needed: Bianca and his mom over there talking to her. "I wonder if Dad wants to play for me for a minute."

"No. Don't do it. There's nothing you can say to make anything better. Plus, Dad hasn't played in a couple of weeks and he's taking care of Benito," Mo said, referring to their little nephew. "Come on, time to finish the match."

Alec's performance was as crappy in the last two chukkas as it had been in the first four. He gave his twin a wide berth when they were in the locker room, showering and changing. He wasn't looking forward to joining his family, who were up on the second-floor balcony of the main barn area. When Diego and Alec had started designing and developing the polo grounds, they'd known they wanted a place for the family to hang out after matches. In fact, Diego was hiring an event manager to run the space as it had become popular with many of the townspeople in Cole's Hill.

When he left the locker room, he went to the barn instead of up to the balcony where everyone was waiting, including Scarlet O'Malley. He wished he had his laptop with him but instead he leaned against Dusty his polo pony's stall, took out his phone, pulled up the internet and deployed the search algorithm that he'd developed to find all imprints left by a person on the web. It wouldn't help him in time for the brunch he was having with Scarlet and his family, but afterward he'd have a better idea of who she was and why she was here.

One night in her bed had whetted his appetite for her but he'd resigned himself to never seeing her or touching her again. There was just too much explaining to do, so he'd figured that she'd just be one of those women he thought about wistfully from afar.

But now she was back and he wanted her, as badly as he had the first time he'd kissed her.

Dusty lifted his head and looked toward the barn entrance. Alec turned and saw Scarlet walking through the doors toward him. He took a deep breath as he pocketed his smartphone.

"Hello."

"Hi, Alejandro. I was waiting for you upstairs," she said.

"Sorry. I wanted to apologize to Dusty for my poor playing today," he said.

She tipped her head to the side and studied him. She didn't say anything, just crossed her arms over her chest and waited.

"What?"

"Nothing. But now I know what you look like when you lie."

He straightened away from the stall and walked toward her. "No, you don't. That's the truth."

"Are you sure? Because you have the exact same look on your face as you did when you introduced yourself to me as Mauricio."

Three

He stood there in the middle of the stables looking more at home than he'd been at the gala in Houston. She wondered if she was glimpsing the real man now. But then how would she know? Since they'd been introduced, he'd done nothing but lie to her.

"I'm sorry I lied to you, Scarlet," he said. "If there had been a chance to tell you the truth I would have, but I got carried away and the last thing on my mind once we got to your hotel room was explaining the rather complicated fact that I had helped my twin out by pretending to be him."

As close as he stood to her she couldn't help but inhale the spicy, outdoorsy aftershave he wore. She closed her eyes. The scent wasn't unpleasant, but she was pregnant and it bothered her the slightest bit.

Damn.

If she got sick in front of him, she was going to throw the biggest, ugliest fit anyone had ever witnessed. She needed the advantage here. She wanted to find out what kind of man he was before she told him about the baby.

She took a few steps back and turned toward the horse stalls that held the polo ponies. She didn't mind horses but hadn't really ever been a great rider. Tara had been the rider in their family. And since their father always insisted on making a competition of everything the two of them had done, they'd quickly decided not to pursue the same passions.

The queasiness subsided as soon as she stepped away from him.

She turned to look back at him over her shoulder. She'd left her sunglasses on when she'd entered the stables and now it was hard to see him. The lenses were very dark, and she couldn't make out his expression.

Maybe that wasn't a bad thing. She skimmed her gaze down his body. He wore a pair of white jeans with a black belt that emphasized his narrow waist and the strength of his legs. He also wore a light-colored button-down shirt and gray blazer. She wished he appeared unkempt or wrinkled. But instead he looked like the sophisticated man she'd thought him to be.

"So you're a tech guy?" she asked.

One side of his mouth lifted in a sort of half smile. "You could say that."

"I just did," she quipped. Something she'd learned from a lifetime of dealing with her father—a man she'd never understood and still didn't really know— was to always stay on her toes.

"Touché."

"What do you do?" she asked.

"I'll be happy to tell you about it over brunch," he said. "Should we go and join the rest of my family?"

"Not yet," she said. "I want to know more about you, Alejandro."

"Fair enough. I want to know more about you as well, Scarlet. I want to know the woman behind the headlines."

She shook her head. No one knew that woman… Well, maybe Tara had, but she was dead. And Billie and Siobahn saw what she wanted them to see. She had never felt comfortable letting someone all the way in. She doubted this man who'd lied to her when they'd first met would be the one.

"That's not how it's going to work," she said. "It's not a tit-for-tat thing. You lied about who you are. I didn't."

He came over and reached out, taking her hand in his. When he lifted it to his mouth and kissed it, a shiver went up her arm and awareness spread throughout her body. Here was a reaction she could understand. Lust. Pure and simple.

"I did lie. I'm incredibly sorry about that. If I could do it over, I would have told you who I was right away. But everything else about that night was me. I wasn't acting like Mo. He's much duller than I am."

He was inviting her to see the humor in the moment and if she hadn't been pregnant, if her family hadn't been the biggest mess on the planet and if she hadn't thought he was a better man, she might be able to laugh. But there was too much riding on this. She didn't want to give birth to another tragic little human who was doomed like Tara or her mom, or to be fair, like herself. And this man had been a ray of hope until she'd realized he wasn't who she thought he was.

"Are you ever going to be able to forgive me?" he asked.

Sincerity radiated from every inch of his body. He might be a great guy. She just didn't know him.

She shrugged. "I don't know."

"At least meet the rest of my family. I think you'll see that I'm not as big of an asshole as you take me for."

He dropped her hand and turned away from her, but she stopped him with her hand on his shoulder.

She couldn't help letting her fingers flex against the rock-hard muscles.

"Did you do it because of who I am?" she asked. It was one thing she needed to have answered before she could move forward.

"What are you talking about?"

"Did you and your brother believe that lying to me didn't matter because you think I'm morally bankrupt?" she asked. It was one of the nicer ways her critics had put it over the years.

"*Dios mio*, Scarlet. Mo and I never discussed you until after it happened. I told him you were enchanting, beautiful and the kind of woman who made me forget everything but being by your side."

She caught her breath. She wanted to believe him. When she looked into his dark chocolate-colored eyes, she hoped it was truth she saw there. But she didn't know him.

She could only reserve judgment for now and tuck that sentiment away. Time would tell if Alejandro Velasquez was a man of honor.

Given that he'd done nothing but think about Scarlet since she'd shown up at the polo match, Alec was glad to be back in the company of his family. Everyone, including Bart and his sister, was milling around by the bar. Normally they'd be seated at the table and eating by now.

They'd waited for him, or more precisely for Scarlet.

As soon as they walked onto the balcony, Bianca and her sisters-in-law, Kinley and Ferrin, turned toward them.

"I should warn you that everyone here is going to be very curious about you," he said to Scarlet. "Also, I'm not sure if you've ever been in a small town before, but it's pretty much like being on a reality TV show without the cameras. Everyone will know who you are in less than a day and they'll want to know why you're here."

"Nice. I'm used to it. You saw how TMZ published those pics of us kissing before we'd even left the ballroom."

"Fair enough. I will say that generally most people are pretty nice here."

"I'll wait and see. I tend to bring out extreme reactions in people," she said.

"What kind—"

"Alec, where have you been? I'm starving but Mom wouldn't let us start eating until you were here with your date," Bianca said, coming up to them. "And it's not nice to keep a pregnant lady away from food."

"Sorry, Bia," he said, leaning over to kiss his sister's cheek. "Have you met?"

"We did earlier. I'm glad you're here," Bianca said to Scarlet. "Now, how about if we mosey over to the buffet line."

She looped her arm through Scarlet's and drew

her toward the food. As the two women walked away, he realized that it might be in his best interest to step back and let his family do their thing. Maybe their warmth and kindness would help convince her that he wasn't a total jerk.

"Mom would scold me if I didn't make sure you're eating, too," he heard Bianca announce as they walked away.

As soon as Bianca and Scarlet were at the buffet table, most of the crowd shifted from their conversations to line up. Mo held back and Alec went over to join his brother.

"So?"

"What?"

"Did you make things right with her?" Mo asked.

"In twenty minutes? It's a wonder that you got Hadley back. I mean you have no clue about women," Alec said.

Mo punched him in the shoulder a little harder than was necessary, but Alec knew his brother was still mad about losing the match to Bart.

"I think I have a bit more than a clue, Alec. After all, one of us will be going home with the woman he loves today, and the other one…"

"Will still be trying to figure out how he screwed up so badly. I don't know what it was about that night," Alec said. "Don't listen to me. I'm tired and have to leave for Seattle in the morning to meet with one of my clients. I'm a little distracted by that."

Mo shook his head at him. "It's not fatigue that made you say that. I get it. It's hard when you screw up. It took me a long time to get past my own anger and realize that I had to change if I wanted Hadley back in my life."

"But you knew she wanted you back," he said.

"Not really," Mo said. "You'll figure this out. Be yourself and see what happens. It's not like all your hookups show up in Cole's Hill. She must be back for a reason."

A reason?

Well, that showed how screwed up he was that he'd never stopped to think about why she had sought him out. Was she in trouble?

She was an heiress with her own reality show and an A-list lifestyle. He doubted she'd come looking for him to solve a problem for her. Maybe she hadn't been able to write off their night together as a onetime thing.

By the time he got his plate of food, there was only one chair left at the table, conveniently between Scarlet and Hadley. He took the seat and noticed that a woman he didn't know was seated across from him. He guessed she must be Scarlet's assistant. She had midnight-black hair that she wore in a ponytail and large sunglasses pushed up on her forehead. When their gazes met, she glared at him.

She was definitely Scarlet's friend. He didn't need to guess how she felt about him. "I'm Alejandro."

"I know," she said.

"And you are?"

"Billie Sampson," she said. "I'm here with Scarlet."

"I guessed," he said. "So are you from New York originally?"

He had learned a long time ago that if he kept asking questions eventually whoever he was talking to would relax.

"No. I'm originally from Maine."

"I have some business interests in Maine," he said. "I need to plan a visit. Can you recommend a time of year?"

"Yes." But she didn't say anything more.

He almost smiled. She was stubborn and he could tell she wasn't going to give him an inch. He respected that. He'd lied to her friend. He liked that Scarlet had someone like Billie in her life.

From what he'd read online, it seemed like her life was a big chaotic mess, but this interaction with Billie and his earlier conversation with Scarlet showed him how little he knew of the real woman.

Billie turned to talk to Ferrin. Alec took a bite of his food before glancing at Scarlet, who was watching him.

"You have a good friend in her," Alec said.

"I know. It takes a lot to tick her off and even more to win her over," Scarlet said.

"Like you?"

"Yes, just like me. It's just that so many people think they know everything about me that I hold my close friends to a different standard," she said. "They really have my back."

"I'm glad to hear that," he said. He wanted to be cool and just make small talk, but he had never been that kind of guy. He was someone who got answers; it was what made him so good at his job. He solved problems and helped companies by researching their digital imprint and finding ways to clean up the bad stuff.

"I'm glad you're glad," she said, a soft smile playing around her lips.

"I stink at small talk," he said.

"You do," she agreed. "What's on your mind?"

"Why did you come to Cole's Hill?"

Her face lost all color and she chewed her lower lip before wrinkling her nose and sort of shaking her head. "I'm not ready to talk to you about that yet."

So it was something… But what?

Scarlet enjoyed meeting the Velasquez family and their friends. During the lunch, Alec took a lot of good-natured ribbing from his family members about pretending to be Mo. Scarlet wished she could laugh about it but she wasn't there yet.

After they were done eating, Alec's nephew, Benito, and Penny, the daughter of Kinley and Nate Caruthers, wanted to ride the ponies, so the group went back downstairs so the kids could ride. Billie was deep in conversation with Ferrin Caruthers, the daughter of illustrious college football coach Gainer.

"Hey, Scarlet, come over here," Hadley called out.

She sat down next to Hadley, who was engaged in an intense conversation with her sister and her sister's fiancé. Hadley leaned closer to Scarlet. "So, I figure you and I are the only ones who don't think the fact that Mo and Alec switched places is funny."

"Yeah. I mean I get that this family likes to joke but it was kind of a dumb thing for grown men to do," Scarlet said.

"I agree. Do you know why they did it?"

"No. Alec has promised to tell me when we're alone," she said.

"Well, it's totally Mo's fault. You should know that to begin with. He got sick with food poisoning and didn't want to cancel. So, he asked Alejandro to accept the award for him, and read the prepared speech."

"It sounds so reasonable when you say it like that," she said softly, almost to herself.

"It does. But, of course, I saw the photo of the two of you kissing and I thought it was Mo. He and I have some history, so it caused problems for us. Once we talked, I got why they did it, but it still hurt to see his name and yours linked together everywhere on social media," Hadley said. "I think… I can't speak for Alec but once he realized the photo was everywhere, he rushed to Mo to try to fix things. Still, I know that doesn't make him a good guy in your eyes."

Scarlet leaned back in the chair and tipped her head up to stare at the summer sky. It was hot, and she felt sticky and tired. Hearing Hadley's explanation of the lie didn't make her feel better. She was more confused than ever.

Alec should have said something to her at some point that night.

"Thanks for sharing that with me," she said, realizing that Hadley was waiting for a response from her.

"It didn't help, did it?"

"No. I'm still ticked."

"Me, too," Hadley said. "Half the town thinks I took Mo back after he kissed you."

"They think we just kissed?" Scarlet asked.

"Well, probably more, but I'm not giving them any of my time. The thing with Mo and me is more complicated because we have a long relationship. So, I've definitely seen the real guy behind the hottie that everyone in the town thinks he is. I've seen him angry and sad and apologetic. He's real to me. I don't think that Alec is that way for you yet."

"He's not," Scarlet admitted. "I don't know that he ever will be."

"If you need someone to talk to," Hadley said, "I'm here. In fact, I'm hosting book club at the Bull Pen on Friday night if you want to join us."

"What's the Bull Pen? What book are you reading?"

"It's a bar and music hall on the outskirts of Cole's Hill. We never read a book but just call it book club so our moms won't be on us about going out too much. Funny how a weekly book club is fine, but drinks aren't."

Scarlet had to smile at the way Hadley said it. "Who will be there?"

"Let's see. My best friends, Zuri and Belle, and Helena if her fiancé, Malcolm, is working late," Hadley said. "You can bring Billie if you want."

"Let me talk to her and see if she wants to come. My friend Siobahn is here with me, as well," Scarlet said. "Your book club sounds like her kind of thing."

"Great. So, I'll put you down as a maybe." Hadley reached for her phone. "What's your cell? I'll text you, so we can keep in touch."

After Hadley sent her her number, Scarlet realized she was starving. She hadn't been able to eat at the buffet mainly because everyone at the table had been asking her questions and her stomach was in knots. But now she wanted to eat.

"Do you know where I can get something to eat here?"

"I'm heading there now."

"Scarlet, this is my sister, Helena," Hadley said. "Hel, this is Scarlet O'Malley."

"Hello, I love your show. And I have to be honest—you're gorgeous in person," Helena said.

"Thank you," Scarlet said. "Your fiancé is playing with the Velasquez team?"

"Yes," Helena said. "He grew up hanging out with the Velasquez brothers."

"There was tons of food left from the brunch. Come on, I'll show you the kitchen." She followed Hadley and found Bianca was already in there eating a plate of enchiladas.

"Busted," Bianca said. "I'm going to be on a water and carrot stick diet after I give birth but right now I don't even care."

Hadley, Helena and Scarlet laughed with Bianca as she took a huge bite of her food. Scarlet made herself a plate.

Hadley left the kitchen to take a call. Bianca wiped her mouth as Scarlet and Helena sat down next to her and started eating. She was so hungry she ate too quickly, and she didn't realize it until she felt the food start to come back up.

Crap.

Glancing around trying to find the bathroom, she got out of chair, pushing it back too forcefully. Bianca glanced over at her as she tried to be cool and walk out of the room, but she felt the bile in back of her throat and no amount of swallowing was going to keep this down. She looked around and saw the sink. She ran toward it, getting there just as she threw up. This was the worst. She rinsed her mouth and straightened, taking the towel that Bianca was holding out to her and Helena had gotten her a cup of water.

"So... How far along are you?" Bianca asked.

"What are you talking about?" Scarlet knew there was a slim chance that Bianca was going to let her get away with pretending she wasn't pregnant.

"Okay. I guess it was the pork. Sometimes it doesn't agree with me. Especially when I'm meeting new people," Helena said.

"No," she said, not wanting to add another lie to her life right now. "You were right. I'm six weeks... maybe seven. When was that gala in Houston?"

"No wonder you were so upset when you found out he lied," Bianca said.

"Yeah. I'm not sure if I should tell him or not," Scarlet said. "I know you don't know me, but would you mind keeping this between us for now?"

"You have my word," Bianca said. "And my ear if you need a friend."

Scarlet nodded. She hadn't expected to find women like the ones she'd met here in Cole's Hill. No one wanted her social connections or felt the need to be catty; instead they seemed to just accept her as she was.

For the first time in her life, someone else was really depending on her. Not for a paycheck or entrée into another world, but for something way more important. She needed all of the emotional support she could get as she tried to figure out what kind of man Alec was and if he'd be a good father to their unborn child.

Four

This day wasn't going at all the way he planned. And when he felt someone tugging at the hem of his blazer and looked down to see Penny, his five-year-old niece, he knew the surprises weren't over.

"What's up?" he asked as he stooped down to bring himself to her eye level.

"Tio, can girls play polo?" Penny asked.

"Yes, they can," he answered her. "Why do you ask?"

"Daddy said girls can't."

Oh. Polo was a dangerous sport and he could understand why Nate wouldn't want his daughter to play, but he had a feeling Kinley would lose it if she heard that Nate had said *girls* couldn't play.

He figured Nate for a smarter man than that.

"Let's go find your daddy and I'll show him some of the safety equipment that's available. I think he just wants you to be safe," Alec said, standing and taking Penny's hand in his as he walked over to where Nate and Kinley were talking to Bart and some of the other players.

"Daddy, Tio Alec said girls can play polo," Penny announced as they joined the group.

"Did you tell her girls couldn't?" Kinley asked.

"No. I didn't say that. I said she couldn't because it's not safe. I even showed her a video of Zaria playing," Nate said, bending over to look his daughter in the eye. "Didn't I?"

"Yes, Daddy," Penny said. "But Beni can play."

"His uncles are teaching him. And right now, he has to ride with one of them every time," Nate said.

"But I'm a better rider," Penny said.

"Maybe so, scamp, but for right now that's the rule," Nate said, scooping her into his arms and standing up.

"I'm happy to have you ride with me, Penny," Alec said.

"Can I?"

"We'll discuss it at home," Kinley said.

Penny made a face at Kinley and looked very unhappy. "You lied about what Daddy said, girlie. You know that there has to be a consequence."

"I'm sorry, Daddy," Penny said.

As the three of them left the group, Alec noticed Scarlet watching him and realized he had no idea what she expected of him. They were strangers. It didn't matter that he knew about the birthmark on the small of her back just above her buttocks or that he couldn't forget the way her tongue felt in his mouth when they kissed. They were still strangers.

Intimate strangers.

He needed to change that. Well, *need* might be too strong a word, but he wanted to change that. He wanted to know her better and to find out why she was here.

"Ladies," he said as he approached them. "Scarlet, would you like to spend the afternoon with me so we can have a chance to talk?"

Billie stepped closer to Scarlet. Scarlet hugged her friend and then smiled at her. "Why don't you go home and I'll meet you there."

"Sure. But if you change your mind, text me and I'll come and get you."

Billie walked away but not before giving Alec a warning glance.

"I think it's safe to say she doesn't like me," Alec said.

"Yeah, I think so," Scarlet said. "So what did you have in mind?"

"I can give you a tour of the town. We have a nice Main Street with one-of-a-kind boutiques. Or we can take a drive out toward my family's ranch, Arbol

Verde," he said. "Or we can go back to my place and I'll have my housekeeper make us an afternoon snack and we can sit by the pool and talk."

He thought he might be pushing it by inviting her back to his house but he wanted a chance to really be able to talk to her and clear up the mess he'd made. But he didn't want to coerce her or rush her in any way.

"Hmm… I'm not sure," she said.

"I'm not trying to pressure you but I have to go to Seattle in the morning to meet with one of my clients and I'll be gone until Saturday, so if we don't talk today… I'm not sure how long you will be here," he said.

"Fair enough. I've rented a home here temporarily," she said. "After seeing the town, it seems like a good place to invest. It's growing fast and I don't have any property in this part of Texas."

"It is a good place to invest." But something about her interest in buying here didn't ring true. She didn't have a reputation for hanging out in small Texas towns. She was more about big-city, red-carpet events. But he wasn't going to question her. He was simply glad she was here. "So should we go to my place?" he asked.

"Uh, no," she said. "I don't even know you, Alec. I mean, the first time we met you lied about you who you were."

"Fair enough," he said. "I just thought someplace

private might be better so we could talk and get to know each other. But I don't want you to feel uncomfortable. I really screwed up, Scarlet, and if there's anything I can do to make this better, I want to fix it."

"Where is your house?" she asked. "A conversation someplace where we have our privacy might be good."

"I have a house in the newer section of the Five Families neighborhood. I just finished renovating it."

"I'd love to see your home," she said. "My house is in the Five Families, as well."

"It's a really nice community. But I'm sure I don't have to sell you on the amenities. Who was your Realtor?"

"Helena's fiancé. Small world, huh?"

"Definitely. I think I'm related to everyone in this town either by blood or marriage," he said. "And it's not just my family. All of the five families are like that."

"What are the five families?" she asked as they walked to his car. He opened the passenger door of his Maserati and helped her in as he told her about the members of the original five families who'd founded Cole's Hill. His ancestor Javier Velasquez had been a rancher in the area thanks to a land grant from the Spanish king before Jacob Cole, for whom the town was named, settled here with his stepdaughter, Bejamina Little. The other three families were the

Carutherses, whose ancestor Tully Caruthers and his sister, Ethel, had built a house where the Five Families clubhouse stood today; the Abernathys, who'd been rustlers before settling down and becoming ranchers; and the Grahams. Their ancestor had been the undertaker, and his descendants had turned their old ranch on the outskirts of town into a microbrewery.

Cole's Hill had history and charm, and as he drove through the small town toward the Five Families neighborhood she saw families walking together on Main Street. She wanted that for her child. This kind of slow-paced, ideal life. And Alec, even though he'd lied to her, seemed to be a decent guy after all.

The kind of a guy who might even be a good father, but was she simply fooling herself again? Seeing what she wanted to see in him? She wasn't going to take a chance on her child's future. Alec Velasquez was going to have to prove to her the kind of man he was.

Scarlet walked around Alec's pool while he spoke to his housekeeper about preparing some food. Apparently he hadn't had a chance to eat at lunch, either, because his family had been questioning him about her. As far as she was concerned, that was his own fault, so she couldn't muster much sympathy for him.

She took her strappy sandals off and walked barefoot on the pool deck, which was smooth and warm under feet. She took off the hat she'd been wearing at the polo grounds as well, tossing it on the coffee table in the conversation area of the patio. There was a solid stone fireplace, surrounded by a love seat and large armchairs. There was even a dining area in the shade of some large oak trees. The pool was magnificent; it had a two-tiered water feature that kept the water flowing and a separate hot tub in an elevated corner nearby.

The yard was lush and looked like a lush, land-scaped paradise nestled right in the heart of southern Texas. She wasn't sure what she'd expected of Alec... Well, honestly nothing, but this still surprised her. She thought it was because he didn't seem like the kind of guy who'd lie about who he was.

She remembered Hadley's explanation. That Mauricio had been violently ill... And she wanted to believe that was the truth. But she was still hurt. And it didn't explain why Alec hadn't come clean once they'd been together.

It was just one example of the universe having a laugh at her expense. She knew that she was being melodramatic but hey, she was pregnant by a stranger in a town where she really knew only two people, so she felt justified.

She glanced at her watch, wondering what she was doing here. Usually she followed her whims, and though Tara had said that it was the same as following your instinct, Scarlet had never truly believed that. She always felt like she was jumping from one extreme situation to the next.

And this calm and tranquil backyard didn't feel right. It was actually too serene. Too…weird. She needed to hear horns blaring, the thumping base beat of her DJ neighbor trying out some new tracks or even just the sound of Billie talking out loud to herself.

If her intent in coming to Cole's Hill was to find someone to help her decide what to do about her situation, she was pretty sure Alec was the one.

Don't ask for answers if you're not going to listen. Tara's voice danced through her mind.

She just shook her head. She wasn't in the mood to be reasonable.

It would be easier if she saw some signs of Alec's depravity or anything that she could latch on to get mad at him about so she could just leave and then make her own decisions about the baby.

She looked around the backyard. Alec had a nice house. It was the kind of place she would have loved as a child. There was a willow branch tunnel on one side that she and Tara would have loved to explore as girls. The O'Malley gardens had all been formal, laid out in the style of Versailles, so there hadn't been any hidden spots to play.

"Okay, the food is all sorted out. Sorry, but I am definitely one of those people who gets hangry and

I don't want to give you more of a reason to think I'm an asshole."

Turning to face him, she noticed he'd taken off his jacket and rolled up his sleeves, revealing his strong forearms and a smart watch. She knew he worked in tech and Billie thought he was pretty much at the top of his game, but honestly that didn't matter to her. She'd met men who were at the top of the Forbes 400 list but who were morally bankrupt. Though it did ease her mind that he wasn't after her for her money, that wasn't really her concern.

What kind of man is he?

Could he be trusted with a child or would he screw it up?

"Great," she said, walking over to the large swing that faced the willow arbor and sitting down. "I guess there's nothing left for us to do but to talk."

"Of course," he said. He came over to where she sat and hesitated. "May I join you?"

"Yes," she said.

The swing dipped a bit when he sat on the wooden bench and then he leaned back, stretching his arm along the backrest. His fingers were close to the back of her neck but he didn't touch her. That didn't mean that she wasn't incredibly aware of his hand so close to her.

She remembered the way he'd stroked his finger down the side of her neck that night at the awards banquet. He'd been leaning in to make a joke about one of the people at their table who kept bringing up the fact that he'd purchased a Maserati from the factory.

She turned so that she could avoid his touch, hoping that would give her the focus she needed, but instead she realized it put her face-to-face with the man himself. He was sprawled on the seat, looking completely at ease as he set the swing into motion. He'd taken off his sunglasses; she met his dark chocolate gaze and realized at last why she wanted so desperately to find something wrong with Alejandro.

She liked him.

Or to be more precise, she liked what she saw. He moved like a man who was comfortable in his own skin, and that was appealing to her. But also, he just seemed relaxed. Except for that moment when she'd surprised him at the polo match, he'd been calm and unflappable.

She wondered if that would still be the case if he found out that one night with her had more consequences than either of them could have expected.

Alec felt like he hadn't acquitted himself very well with Scarlet. Looking back on the night they'd met, he realized that maybe he'd felt free to be himself because he knew he'd never see her again. There had been no reason to try to impress her or to be anything other than how he really was. For one night it hadn't seemed to matter that he wasn't good at relationships or any of those other things. He could just be himself and he had been. Of course, the irony was to be himself, he'd had to pose as his brother.

Now that she was here at his home, he struggled a little bit to relax. Part of it was that she'd gotten even more beautiful since the last time he'd seen her. He wanted her, and each breath he took just reminded him of the scent of her perfume and how it had lingered on his skin after their night together.

"I guess the best thing to do would be to tell you why I was impersonating my brother," he said, unsure of where to start. But the truth was always a good place. He applied a lot of the same principles he used in his business in his life. Getting all the facts down helped him focus on what steps he needed to take to solve the problem.

"Hadley caught me up on Mauricio being sick and you helping him out. Neither of us could figure out why two grown men wouldn't just mention the fact that they'd switched places," she said.

There was an edge to her tone that he couldn't ignore. She was pissed and he didn't blame her.

"Honestly, it just seemed easier since it was so last-minute for me to show up and accept his award without alerting the organizers," he said at last. It had been easier; that way he didn't have to answer questions about his company or talk about his own work. Being Mo was like wearing a mask. His brother was known for his gregarious personality so it had been a chance for Alec to let his guard down.

In fact, Scarlet might not have noticed him at all if he'd been there as Alec.

"I get that. But why didn't you say anything to me?" she asked.

He took a deep breath and looked away from her toward the pool, watching the sun dance on the water for a few minutes before he finally answered. "It just never occurred to me after the dinner. I didn't expect to have that connection with you, and by the time I realized you didn't know who I really was, it would have been ridiculous to tell you."

"Why ridiculous?" she asked. "Because I was just a hookup?"

No, but he wasn't about to tell her the truth. That he'd started to like her and didn't want her to be disappointed. He hadn't wanted the night to end and it would have if he'd mentioned he'd been lying about who he was.

"To be honest I wasn't really thinking that night and it wasn't until we were in your hotel room… Anyway, I'm sorry. I should have told you as soon as things started to be more than just two people at a banquet table chatting."

She arched her eyebrow at him and then crossed her arms under her breasts, which looked fuller and larger than he remembered from that night.

"Yes, you should have," she said. "So… Why didn't you call me the next day?"

"I was pretty much trying to keep my brother from killing me and then you'd checked out of the hotel and I wasn't sure how to word an email."

She didn't say anything else as she took her sunglasses from the top of her head and put them back on her face. She shifted on the swing and he felt the brush of her hair against his hand. He wished he could go back in time and start the evening they met with the truth. She had him tied in knots. They were strangers. Strangers with anger between them, and he couldn't blame her for being mad.

He did seem to really suck at personal relationships. Give him a computer keyboard and an empty room and he could wow anyone via videoconference or online chat but this face-to-face interaction he always managed to screw up.

"I have to tell you something," she said.

"Okay," he said.

"It's probably not something you are going to want to hear but you need to," she said. "What do you know about my family?"

He knew a little bit thanks to online searches. He'd also run an algorithm to compile some of the results of a deeper search but he hadn't had a chance to read them. And he knew it would be better to hear about her family from her rather than to read about it online.

"Some. I mean I know you're part of the O'Malley Brewing family. I know that you have banking interests here and in Europe. I think you have a sister—"

"Had. She died eighteen months ago," she said.

"I'm sorry for your loss," he said.

"Thanks," she said. "Do you know anything about my dad?"

He shrugged. He wasn't sure what kind of relationship she had with her old man but there was no way Alec was going to say that he seemed to be immature and selfish from the press reports. The man was on his fourth or fifth wife and Alec was pretty sure he'd read that the latest Mrs. O'Malley was eighteen.

"It's okay. You can say it. He's got an eye for younger women," Scarlet said. "My family isn't like yours, Alejandro. I was raised with nannies and in boarding schools. I'm used to doing everything by myself and being on my own."

Alec wasn't sure where she was going with this. "There were times I wished I wasn't a twin."

"I can imagine. Your family does seem very comfortable getting into each other's business."

"That's true," he said.

"I'm sure you're wondering why I brought up family, and there is no easy way to say this…" She paused, and the look on her face made him brace for the worst. "I'm pregnant. And my family isn't the nurturing kind. I thought the man I'd slept with was

Humanitarian of the Year and maybe he'd be a good parent but now I'm not sure."

He put his foot down, abruptly stopping the motion of the swing, and looked over at her not sure he'd heard her correctly. Pregnant? He wasn't ready to be a father. He didn't even know Scarlet. Sure, he wanted to get to know her…but a baby?

His baby?

Someone like his sweet nephew, Benito. A child who could be the best parts of the both of them.

A baby.

A baby!

"Are you sure?" he asked.

"Would I be here if I wasn't?" she asked.

"No I guess not. I'm… I have never thought of having kids other than in the abstract. In fact, we only slept together that one time—are you sure it's mine?"

Five

Was she sure it was his?

What the f—

Did he honestly think she'd come to Texas just to trap him? "Honestly, I've never been so insulted."

"Fair enough, but as you said it's not like we know each other or that we were even in a relationship."

He sounded so reasonable and she knew he was justified to ask questions. But she'd been dealing with a bunch of crap and she wanted just once to have a man step up and not look for an out. She shook her head.

"I don't have a DNA test in my bag but I'm happy to take one," she said. "It's odd that you think of all the men I know you'd be my first choice to approach with my news if I weren't absolutely certain."

He shifted back against the seat of the swing and she noticed how his jaw tightened. She braced herself for an angry outburst. She'd read about his twin and that he was known for his hot temper and inability to control it.

"You're right. You weren't even coming to see me, were you?" he asked, standing up and walking a few feet from the swing. He put his hands on his hips and stared across his large backyard; and she noticed his head was bowed slightly.

He was complicated, this twin whom she didn't know. And she realized she had been a bit touchy about the paternity of the baby, but it was one of her hot buttons. She got up and went over to him, putting her hand on the small of his back.

"A lot of the more salacious reports about me like to paint me as a carbon copy of my father—someone who's insatiable when it comes to the opposite sex, jumping from bed to bed—but there isn't much I can do about it. Still, it does bother me," she said. "To be fair my reaction to the news of this pregnancy was very similar to yours. It was only one time. But as my doctor said, that's all it takes."

"Yeah, I know. I never meant to insult you," Alec said. He turned to face her and one side of his mouth quirked in a tentative smile. "Seems I owe you another apology."

"Apology accepted," she said. He wasn't what she expected. There was a humbleness and sincerity to him that she'd seldom encountered.

"Alec, would you and your guest like something to eat?" his housekeeper asked.

"Are you hungry?" he asked Scarlet in turn.

"I'm not, but if you are, please eat," she said.

"I always have a snack after a polo match," he said. "Please bring it out to the dining area, Rosa."

"*Si*, Rosa," he said, then spoke to her in Spanish.

Scarlet had only a rudimentary knowledge of the language, but she understood as he thanked Rosa for the food and told her that she could take the rest of the afternoon off to enjoy with her family.

Rosa smiled at him and put the tray on the table in the dining area under the trees.

"I asked Rosa to bring drinks for us… O'Malley's Blonde Brew. But now I'm thinking you'd prefer juice or water?"

"Water would be great," she said.

He gestured for her to go and have a seat at the table while he went to the bar area and opened a small refrigerator that had been built into the river stone.

As she sat down, she realized that this pregnancy situation was more complicated than she'd considered. Obviously, her first priority was to make sure that the child had a parent who loved her and put her first, but now there was more that she hadn't thought of.

She'd never considered he'd suspect she was lying about him being the father. She supposed his suspicion was fair enough, but it raised more questions. She would have to be careful where she had the test. She wasn't ready for the public to know about this pregnancy, not until she decided what she was going to do. The tabloids would have a field day with this story.

She didn't want her child to grow up with the stain of all the mistakes and tragedies that had dogged her life. She wanted a more protected upbringing for the child. The kind of childhood that a place like Cole's Hill and a family like the Velasquezes could provide.

She wanted the baby to have the kind of family that Alec seemed to have. But she knew firsthand that appearances could be deceiving.

"You look very pensive," he said.

"Wow. That's not a word I usually hear applied to me."

"I expect you're more used to *sexy, glamorous, trendsetting*," he said.

She shrugged. She'd cultivated an image for herself and a lifestyle to fill the emptiness left by the death of her mother and her father's distance.

"Maybe. What words would describe you, Alec?" she asked. It was time to stop dwelling on what she knew—she wasn't an ideal candidate to become a mother—and find out if he had the qualities to be a good father.

"I want to say dangerous, sexy—of course—and I'm… That's where it breaks down. Honestly, I'm reliable. And tenacious—I can't let things go. Also, according to my brothers, I'm a sore loser."

She laughed at that. "I am, too. I don't see the point in pretending I'm okay with losing. If I compete I'm doing it to win."

He nodded, moving the cloche off the tray and pulling his plate toward him. She noticed that it was nachos. "Do you mind if I eat? Are you sure you don't want anything?"

"I think you better. Don't want to see you hangry. I'm okay," she said, realizing that she sort of liked this man. She wasn't going to rush to judgment because there was a lot about him she didn't know. But he'd been honest with her today, and after the big lie that had started their…well, relationship… she needed that.

She sipped her water while they exchanged opinions on books, music, TV and movies. He did everything digital—watched it all on apps.

"But I do have a library in my house," he added. "As much as I prefer the convenience of digital, I like seeing books on my shelves."

She did, too. She was surprised at how much they had in common. It gave her hope that he might be the solution she'd been searching for.

"What else do you prefer?"

"Not lying to you," he said.

"Me, too," she said. "I'd like to see more of this place."

"I'm done here," he said. "Let's go."

He offered her his hand, and when she took it, a shiver went up her arm. She wanted to be smart about this thing with Alec. Keep it all about the baby. But a part of her liked him and still wanted him.

After he ate, Alec took her on a tour of his gardens. His mind was roiling with so many different thoughts it was hard to focus.

He'd never been so careless in his dating life. But to be honest there was something about Scarlet that was different from any other woman. There had been a spark when he'd first been introduced to her at the gala and it hadn't lessened at all over time.

"Scarlet isn't a typical Irish name, is it?" he asked as they strolled down a path lined by rosebushes in full bloom.

"No, Not at all. My mom picked our names. She loved *Gone with the Wind*. She loved how it was the strength of the women that kept everything going. She wanted my sister and me to have that same strength. So she named Tara after the plantation and me after Scarlett O'Hara. She never really liked Melanie so that wasn't an option."

"I love that. I've never read *Gone with the Wind*," he admitted.

Scarlet shook her head, her long blond hair brushing her shoulders as she smiled over at him. "Me neither. But I have seen the movie numerous times."

Suddenly, the smile left her face and he realized that there was more to the story. Should he push or just let it be? He wanted to know more but he was actually enjoying not being in constant conflict with her. He didn't want to have to apologize again.

"My brothers and I are all named after our ancestors," he said.

"That's nice," she said. Then, without missing a beat, she blurted, "What are we going to do about this baby?"

This baby.

Not our baby or her baby. This baby. Was she trying to figure out what kind of man he was before she included him in her life and the baby's life?

Was he reading too much into her word choice?

"I don't know. I think if you aren't opposed we'll have a DNA test," he said.

"I'm not opposed. It will make my lawyers happier, as well. I'm not scheduled to start shooting my reality show again until late October," she said. "I'd like to keep this quiet until then."

"That suits me. I do have to go to the West Coast in the morning. It's not something I can put off. Will you be here when I get back? I don't mind coming to New York to see you. Mauricio and Hadley have a place there that I can use as my base."

"I think I'll stay here," she said. "For now."

"I'll leave you the numbers for my sister and Hadley, so you aren't alone," he said.

"I have Billie and another friend here with me, and Hadley already gave me her number," Scarlet said.

"That's good," he said. She realized he was mentally going through some list and he'd switched from being relaxed into some sort of business mode. It was interesting to watch.

"Also, I was invited to book club with Hadley and her sister so I have that to look forward to," she said.

"Book club? You know they just go to a bar and hang out, right?"

"I do." She waited to see if he was going to try to tell her not to go.

"I guess that sounded a bit judgy."

"Yeah, just a bit," she said. "One thing you should know about me, Alec, I'm not stupid. I play a role for my reality show and social media but that's not really me."

"I get that. I sort of clean up the online profiles of large companies and people in the public eye who stand to lose a lot if their image doesn't jibe with the expectation of who they are," he said. "I never thought you were stupid, Scarlet."

"What do you think about me?" she asked.

"You've never said. I mean I know I shocked the heck out of you by showing up here, but beyond that, I don't know what you think."

"That's a loaded question," he said, stopping in the middle of the willow branch arbor and turning to face her.

The scent of jasmine was strong here; she realized that someone had woven the climbing vine into the willow branches above their head.

"Is it?" she asked.

Because it seemed straightforward to her.

"Si," he said.

She noticed he switched between English and Spanish without really seeming to think about it. She liked it. She thought it happened only when he was distracted.

This close she couldn't help but notice the light stubble on his jaw, which drew her gaze to his mouth. He had firm, full lips that she knew felt just right pressed against her. She felt a jolt of desire go through her and blinked, taking a step back.

She hadn't come here to hook up again.

He was the father of her child and that was complicated enough. But she'd never been one to walk away from something she wanted, and frankly, she wanted Alec Velasquez.

She put her hand on his chest, running her finger over the skin exposed by the buttons he'd left undone at his collar. She touched his gold chain and lifted it up to examine the medallion. He hadn't been wearing this the night they met.

"Tell me what you're thinking, Alejandro," she said softly, hearing the lust in her own voice and knowing she'd made no attempt to disguise it from him.

His put his hand over hers, pressing it flat against his chest as he leaned in, angling his head to one side, never breaking eye contact with her as he brought his mouth closer to hers.

"I'm thinking that if I don't kiss you I might die," he admitted. Then his mouth brushed over hers as his hand tangled in her hair.

She sighed, realizing that this was what she'd been waiting for and that it had been worth the wait.

The tension that had been in his gut since he'd first seen her this morning at the polo grounds finally eased. He put his hands on either side of her neck, holding her gently, reminding himself that she was pregnant, and this kiss could be the start of something.

It was hard to keep the embrace gentle, hard to rein in his desire for her, because the kiss simply whetted his appetite for more. It made him want to lift her into his arms and carry her into the house and up to his bedroom.

Memories of their night together stirred in his mind, and now that he was touching her again he wanted more. But he was determined to keep things cool and casual. He didn't know what the future held for them. And really, he probably shouldn't be kissing her.

But she'd touched him and teased him, and he'd never really had to deny himself anything he wanted.

And damn, she tasted so good that none of that mattered. He opened his mouth over hers and their tongues clashed. She sighed as she moved her hands to his waist, holding him even closer. It was all he could do to keep from crushing her against his body. To keep from escalating this beyond a simple kiss to something hot and heavy.

His cock stirred, and he shifted his hips back so she wouldn't rub against his erection. But she pulled him closer with her hands on his waist, rubbing her center against him, and he couldn't help but thrust against her. She moaned deep in her throat and changed the angle of her head so that he could deepen the kiss.

He did, taking everything she offered him. He'd spent every moment since their night together reliving it and wanting to be back in her arms. Now she was here.

Yes, it was complicated, but that didn't seem to matter when he had her in his arms. He rubbed his finger up and down the column of her neck and felt the shiver that went through her as she wrapped her arms around his waist and cupped his butt, drawing him closer to her. She lifted one thigh and wrapped it around his hips. He groaned and got even harder, though he hadn't thought that was possible.

He rubbed himself against her as he continued the kiss. But he knew that the smart thing would be to break this embrace and step back. He was leaving in the morning. He couldn't sleep with her again and then leave.

That was a bad precedent to set. Yet backing away also didn't feel right.

He lifted his head and rubbed his lips over hers before he broke all contact. "You make me forget everything, even my name."

She shook her head. "You're too clever for that. I doubt a kiss could have that powerful of an effect on you."

He took her hand and drew it down to his erection and she rubbed her hand over him. "You have a very pronounced effect on me."

She stroked him through his pants, tipping her head back so their eyes met. "I seem to."

There was no way to talk about this. He was overwhelmed with the urge to get inside her. He hesitated, though, not wanting her to feel pressure, but then felt her slowly lowering the zipper of his trousers. Her hand slipped inside his open fly.

There was no turning back. He lifted her off her feet and she wrapped her legs around his hips as he carried her out of the willow arbor to the shaded double lounger next to the pool.

He sat down, so she straddled his lap and shifted against him, pushing her hands into his hair and bringing her mouth down on his.

God, he tasted better than she remembered. Straddling his lap made her realize how desperately she wanted to get closer to him. Wanted him close enough so she could feel him inside her. His mouth…damn those perfect lips that felt just right under hers. And the taste of him. It was addicting.

But she could control it.

She kissed him again, even deeper than before, rocking her hips and rubbing her center over the ridge of his erection. It felt so good.

She lifted her head. His eyes were half closed. Rubbing her fingers along his jaw, she felt the abrasion of his stubble, and it sent shivers through her as she shifted around and brought her mouth back to his.

He tasted so good.

She never wanted to stop kissing him. She remembered what it had been like—the sex between them. It had been hard to wake up alone and realize she'd never have him again.

Now she was back in his presence and less than a few hours later she was straddling him, kissing him like she'd never get enough of him.

Addict.

The word echoed in her mind. She pushed herself off him, stumbling back away from him. She wasn't her sister or her mother. She was always in control of her desires.

Until now.

Until Alejandro Velasquez.

She put her hand on her mouth and turned away from him, not saying anything. She heard his heavy breathing and a few minutes later she heard his zipper as he did it up.

"I should be going. Have a safe trip," she said.

"I'll drive you," he said.

"You don't have to," she said.

"I do. It's late July in Texas and I'm a gentleman no matter what you might believe. It's the least I can do."

She nodded and went to find her shoes. As he led her to his car, neither of them said a word about what had happened. And when he pulled into the drive of her rented house, she bolted out as soon as he brought the car to a stop.

She didn't look back but didn't have to because in her mind she still saw the passion on his face when she'd straddled him and she knew that staying away from him was going to be harder than anything she'd ever done.

Six

Scarlet needed to go out and surround herself with people who just wanted her to be the edgy heiress. Alec had somehow found a way to make her remember all the things that she was usually much better at ignoring. Stuff like how much she had missed him… but more than that, how she missed a genuine connection with someone.

"Billie? Siobahn?"

Her little miniature dachshund came trotting into the foyer and Scarlet leaned down to scoop her up. Lulu burrowed into her neck the way she liked and Scarlet closed her eyes as she rubbed her dog's back. Then she set Lulu back on the tile floor and the dog dashed off for the kitchen. She followed Lulu and found Siobahn sitting at the counter, shoulders hunched, staring intently at her smartphone screen.

"Siobahn? You okay?"

"Yeah, I'm good. I can't believe this. Now they're saying it's going to be the wedding of the century," Siobahn said, scrolling on her screen.

Scarlet went over and took the phone from her friend, putting it on the counter behind her. "As if. It might be the tackiest wedding ever but that's it."

Siobahn smiled. "Probably all pink and frothy."

"Definitely. That woman has an unhealthy obsession with tulle."

"She does," Siobahn said. "Where have you been?"

She grabbed two Fiji waters from the fridge and passed one to her friend. "I was meeting with the guy I hooked up with when I came to Houston."

"That Mauricio guy?"

She wrinkled her brow. "Uh, well, it turns out that it was actually his twin brother, Alejandro."

"Ooh. Interesting," Siobahn said, moving over to the padded bench in the breakfast nook and patting the seat next to her.

Scarlet went over and sat next to her friend. She rested her elbows on the wooden table and held the water bottle suspended between her hands.

Interesting.

"Is he why we're in this town no one's ever heard of?" Siobahn asked.

"You needed to get out of the city, too," Scarlet said. She hated to make it seem like she was selfish and did things just in her own best interests. "But yeah."

"You're right. I did need a break," Siobahn agreed. "So tell me what's going on with this guy."

"I'm pregnant," she said without further hesitation, even though the words still stuck in her throat as she said them. It wasn't getting any easier to tell people. She wondered if it ever would or if her kid would be thirty and she'd still feel this foreign, *what-the-fuck* feeling in her gut.

"What? I thought you were super careful," Siobahn said.

"I am normally but I had run out of pills. I figured I'd be fine since I've been on the pill forever and I don't hook up that much. Especially when I'm filming. I figured I'd be okay," she repeated.

"Did he use a condom?"

"Yes…well, one time," she admitted.

"Why am I just now hearing about this?" Siobahn asked. "Sounds like you had one hell of a night."

"We did," she admitted. "Then, of course, he was gone in the morning and I moved on. I like being able to do that. Not get too tied down, but then this…" She looked down at her body. How had this happened? Why now?

"Why did he bolt?"

"Turns out he was impersonating his brother

who was in love with a girl, and he had to get back to Cole's Hill to make things right between them," Scarlet said.

Siobahn looked over at her.

"Seriously?"

"Yeah," Scarlet said, taking a long swallow of her water and wishing it were something stronger. If there was ever a moment she wanted to get drunk and forget everything about her life, it was right now.

"You know you're making me feel better about my sucky life," her friend said, wrapping her arm around Scarlet's shoulder and hugging her.

"That was my main objective," Scarlet joked.

Siobahn smiled. "Do we have the suckiest taste in men ever or has the quality of men in the dating pool just gone significantly downhill?"

"Might just be karma," Scarlet said.

"It might be," Siobahn admitted. "Be nice if the universe had given us a free pass for all the crap things we'd done when we were too dumb to know better."

"It would be. Guess it doesn't work that way, though," Scarlet said.

"Girl, what are you going to do about the baby?" Siobahn asked, looking over at her with those wide eyes that had helped make her so famous.

"I don't know. You know O'Malleys make horrible parents. There isn't one in my direct line who didn't screw up their kids," Scarlet said.

"Yeah, but you're—"

"Please don't say *different*," Scarlet said. "I'm not. I just hide the ugly, selfish bits of myself better than Tara did, and my father does."

"Whatever you decide, I've got your back," Siobahn said. "So, what about Mauri—wait, not Mauricio, Alejandro? Did you tell him about the kid? Or are we keeping this just between us for now?"

"I told him but I'm not sure what's on his mind. He wants me to have a DNA test," Scarlet said.

"Bastard. He didn't believe you?"

"Karma. I have slept with a lot of guys," Scarlet admitted. Granted she'd been in her very early twenties and trying to exorcise some ghosts back then.

"Yeah, but still, why would you try to trap him?"

"I said as much. And once he realized I didn't know who he actually was when I came to town he admitted as much. I'm still going to do it. I need it for my lawyers, but beyond that... I was hoping he'd be a decent guy who would raise the kid."

"Good idea," Siobahn said. "Aside from impersonating his twin, is he a good guy?"

That was the million-dollar question. She shrugged, and luckily Billie walked in before she had to answer any more of Siobahn's questions.

"You two okay?" Billie asked.

Scarlet nodded even though she wasn't okay. She was pregnant and the father of her child wasn't who she'd thought he was. But he also wasn't a bad guy.

She had no real idea what to do next but at lease she had her friends to pleasantly distract her for now.

They spent the evening playing a trivia game and not talking about her pregnancy. But when she went to bed all she could think about was how it had felt to be in Alec's arms.

Helena kept up the smiles until she and Malcolm were in the car. She was thinking about Scarlet and how someone who seemed to have it all was still struggling with her own issues. It sort of drove home how nothing in life was ever easy. It had been nice watching the polo match with her sister and her friends, but it wasn't lost on her that her fiancé had spent most of the time avoiding her. Sure, he'd been cool about it but she knew him well enough, or thought she did, to see that he was trying to avoid her.

He had started to lose a ridiculous amount of weight. She had believed he was taking steps to control his gambling addiction, but here he was hiding something from her again. It was hot in the car and Malcolm fiddled with the air-conditioning as he got in.

"That was a nice day," Malcolm said as he put the vehicle in gear and pulled out of the parking lot of the polo grounds. The parking lot was emptying out. Sometimes if they had a match on Saturday they'd have a party that went into the night but not on Sunday.

Most of the locals in Cole's Hill were still ranch people who had to get up early to care for their livestock. Even Helena had an early day tomorrow. She had to take one of her clients' books to Houston for review by a private accounting firm. It was just routine but she wasn't looking forward to the drive during rush-hour traffic. And she knew being in the car alone would give her too much time to think about Malcolm and wonder what the heck was going on with him.

She took a deep breath. Could she just sweep this under the rug? Could she just play it nice and easy? No. More like hell no. That just wasn't her way.

"Was it? Because it seemed to me that every time I joined a group you were part of you dashed away. What's up?"

"Helena. That's not what was happening," he said. But there was that edge to his voice. The one that she'd become way too familiar with ever since their engagement party. Then they'd had a few weeks of relative normalcy after he'd confessed his gambling problem and how he'd overextended his finances to try to impress her.

"Then tell me what is," she said. "Pull over here and talk to me. I can't do this again, Malcolm. As humiliated as I'd be by calling off the wedding, I will do it if you aren't communicating with me."

He cursed but she heard the clicking of the blinker as he pulled onto the shoulder and put the car in Park. He put both of his arms on the steering wheel and didn't turn to face her.

"I've stopped," he said angrily.

He was pissed. But that was okay because she was, too. "I'm not making an idle threat or trying to manipulate you, Mal. If the prospect of us getting married is causing you stress, then let's just keep living together. If it's something else, then tell me. Two heads are better than one to solve a problem, right?"

He looked over at her and she saw so much turmoil on his face that her heart ached for him. And it ached for herself if she were honest. This was the man she loved. She'd loved him for longer than he knew, and she wanted to have that picture-perfect engagement and wedding and then a long life with him. She didn't want to call things off. Not just because of her ego but because he was the man she wanted. With all his problems and fears, he still was the man who owned her heart.

"Fine. I'm struggling, Hel. It's harder than I thought not to make a bet. I keep thinking of the money we've got as our nest egg and how I could double it—I know I can't do that. I know that one bet won't be enough and that there's no such thing as a sure thing, but at the same time I wake up at two in the morning and plot out ways to increase our money by placing bets."

She sighed. "I know it's not easy for you. Would it help if I made a cost analysis?"

It helped her. But she was an accountant and liked looking at a spreadsheet. Watching the way that her investments would grow soothed her. It always reassured her.

He smiled at her, his real smile, and she felt the love she had for him swell inside. "No, honey, I don't think a spreadsheet would help, but thanks. You're so sexy I always forget what a nerd you are."

She mock-punched his shoulder. "Hey. I'm not a nerd."

"You are, but I love you," he said, turning toward her and reaching out to pull her into an awkward hug because of the seat belts. "I love you more than you know, Helena. I don't want to screw up again."

She reached down and undid both of their seat belts and then hugged him closer before putting her hands on his jaw and looking him in the eyes. "We are both going to screw up a million times during our life. The thing to remember is that I'm here when you do and I'm counting on you to be here when I do."

He kissed her then, and the passion that had always burned between them ignited. She remembered their first time, which had been in a car after the homecoming football game her senior year of high school.

Someone drove by and honked and she pulled back as Malcolm waved at the car. "Guess we should remember we aren't in high school now," he said, laughing.

"Guess so," she said, as they both put their seat belts back on.

Instead of putting the car in gear, he turned to face her. "I'm not going to give in to the impulse to gamble, honey. It's hard and I definitely feel the struggle every day, but I never give in because I know that if I do, it's the path away from you. And I don't think my life would be anything without you."

She squeezed his hand. They'd get through this together, she thought.

As Alec drove back to his house after dropping Scarlet off, he heard the emptiness all around him. Normally that didn't bother him, as he liked solitude, but as he went into his office and pulled up the files that his algorithm had compiled about Scarlet, he realized he felt lonely.

But there was no reason for that. He texted his brothers to see if they were up for a game of pool or something but they both were busy with their women. Diego's wife was in town and since she split her time between Texas and London, Diego wasn't about to blow off an evening with her to hang out with his little brother.

Mo and Hadley were in that honeymoon phase of their relationship, so even though Mo had texted back that Alec was welcome to join them for dinner, the last thing he wanted was to spend an evening feeling like a third wheel.

Instead he sat down at his computer and started reading the files he'd collected on Scarlet. It was interesting to him how much of her life was available online. It went all the way back to her birth and childhood, as her mother had been a model and her father one of the richest men in the United States around the time she was born. He looked at all of the pictures of her online. She had grown up…well, in a very public way and he had to wonder if she'd come to Cole's Hill to see if he was a private man.

She didn't want the spotlight to follow her child around. She knew how impossible it was to grow up that way.

He couldn't postpone his trip to Seattle. His client needed him and one of the things that Alec prided himself on was delivering what his clients required. But one of the main things he noticed about Scarlet was that she'd been left by herself a lot. And now she didn't even have her sister, who had died not that long ago. He wasn't the wisest man when it came to reading the opposite sex but he thought that spending a week away from her when she was feeling so vulnerable might not be the best idea.

He didn't want to make another mistake when it came to Scarlet. They'd seemed to really connect yesterday and she was expecting his child. They needed to find common ground.

Deciding on a course of action, he got in his car and drove back to Scarlet's house. The ride took only five minutes as they lived in the same gated community. When he rang the doorbell, he heard the sound of barking and then voices before the door opened.

Scarlet stood there with the famous singer Siobahn Murphy and Billie, who didn't look any friendlier than she had earlier. A miniature dachshund rushed forward and Alec bent down, holding his hand out to the dog, who sniffed it, then licked him and danced around his feet as he stood back up.

"Alec, I wasn't expecting to see you again before your trip," Scarlet said.

"I know. I've just been thinking that maybe we should spend some more time together and wondered if you'd like to go with me to Seattle," he said. "I have a private plane so that's not an issue."

"She has one, too," Billie said.

"Great. Either way. I have a nice house in Bellevue…" He trailed off, not sure what else to say.

"Let me think about it. When do you need to know?" she asked.

"In the next two hours. I was planning to leave in the morning," he said.

She nodded, then bent down to scoop up the little dog, who was standing on her back legs and looking up at Scarlet. He watched her closely, still wondering what had caused her to leave him so abruptly earlier. Had he rushed her? Was he rushing her now?

Alec just wanted to do the right thing for her. She was pregnant, and she said the baby was his. He was beginning to realize she wasn't the kind of woman who would have come to see him if she wasn't positive he was the father. He wanted to get to know her. His online research had helped but that was her digital imprint; it wasn't necessarily the true picture of her.

"I'll just—"

"Oh, come in," Siobahn said, holding her hand out to him. "I'm Siobahn."

"Alec Velasquez," he said, shaking her hand and stepping into the foyer. He closed the door behind him as Billie shook her head and walked away.

"Go think about if you want to go," Siobahn said to Scarlet. "I'll keep Mr. Velasquez company."

"Please call me Alec," he said.

Scarlet chewed her bottom lip. "Okay, but be nice."

"Of course I will be," Alec said.

"I wasn't talking to you," Scarlet said as she turned to walk down the hall.

"We can talk in here," Siobahn said, leading the way into the formal living room.

Friends of Alec's parents had previously owned this house and he noted that nothing had changed since he'd last been here. He sat on the love seat and Siobahn took the armchair adjacent to him.

"So you don't know if you're the dad?"

Well, she certainly got right to the point. He wasn't prepared to be grilled but given the fact that she was facing a lot of unknowns from him, maybe her friends were justified. But he still hadn't had a chance to make things right with Scarlet before he started answering questions from her friends. "Uh… I felt like it was a legitimate question to ask. I mean there was only that one night and I hadn't heard from her since then," Alec said. "But after we talked I realized that's not the kind of woman she is."

Siobahn leaned back in her chair, crossing her arms over her chest. "What kind of woman is she?"

He didn't want to talk about his feelings for Scarlet. End of story. He wasn't that kind of chatty guy. He didn't know how to put it into words. But for all her flashiness there was something sweet and, odd as it sounded, innocent about her.

He chose his next words carefully, aware that her friend was ready to defend Scarlet if he said anything she didn't like. He would be upset about this mini-grilling he was getting from Siobahn but he couldn't fault her. He'd do the same for his brothers. He was quickly realizing that Scarlet had created a family for herself and their bond was stronger than any she had with her blood relatives.

"She's an enigma so I can't even begin to say that I know her. But she seems honest to me."

"She is. She's got a big heart, buddy, so don't dick around with her," Siobahn said.

"I won't," he said.

"Good," Siobahn said, then stood up. "Just because she looks tough doesn't mean she is."

Siobahn walked out of the room, and a few minutes later he heard Scarlet in the hall. "I'll go with you," she said as she entered the living room. "I'll have Billie drive me to your house in the morning and then we can take your plane. I want to bring Lulu. Will that be okay?"

"Who's Lulu?" he asked.

"My dog," she said.

"That's fine. I'll see you then," he said.

He left her house feeling much better this time. He didn't overanalyze it but he knew that going to her had been the right thing for both of them. Neither of them was sure about this pregnancy or each other and they needed all the time they could find together to learn to trust each other.

Seven

Alec parked his Maserati in the garage at the airport reserved for him the next morning and then got out to open Scarlet's door, but she was already standing there with Lulu on a leash when he came around the car. So he tried to be cool and pivoted to the trunk to unload his computer bag and one of Scarlet's suitcases. The others were in the car that Billie was driving.

He wasn't sure if her friend and assistant was joining them, and frankly he hoped she wasn't because he wanted to get to know Scarlet on her own. But he wasn't in a position to make demands. He knew that so he was willing to wait and see what Scarlet had in mind.

She wore a pair of moto-style leggings and a long T-shirt with a picture of Audrey Hepburn in her iconic *Breakfast at Tiffany's* role. She arched one eyebrow at him and he realized he had been staring.

"You have great legs," he said. "I'm not going to pretend I didn't notice them and wasn't staring."

She shook her head. "Are you always this blunt?"

"Yes. Which is why I seldom socialize."

"I like it," she said, walking toward him with her large bag on her shoulder and the little dog walking along beside her. "Once Billie drops off my suitcase, we can leave. I have a tiny crate for Lulu to stay in during takeoff and landing. She likes to burrow in her blanket in the crate."

"That's fine," he said. "I could have taken my truck instead of the sports car to accommodate your luggage."

"It's okay. Is that all you packed?" she asked, gesturing to his computer bag.

"I have a home in Seattle so I don't need to bring clothing back and forth with me. And I keep a limited wardrobe on the jet, as well."

"I'm fascinated with your life," she said. "What is it you do that requires you to have houses all over…? Is it just the United States or are you global?"

They had stepped out of the garage and were standing on the tarmac when Billie pulled up next to them.

"Global. Just leave your luggage on the tarmac

and I'll have it collected," he said. "Do you need this bag with you during the flight?"

"No," she said.

He nodded and turned to walk to the jet where the attendants were waiting. He employed a staff of five who rotated during the month. He had the two pilots and then three attendants depending on what was necessary on different flights.

"Please stow the luggage and then we're going to need to figure out the best place for a dog crate," he said. "It needs to be stabilized during takeoff and landing."

"Yes, sir. Will you be accompanied by the two ladies?" Marg, the head flight attendant, asked.

"I don't know," he admitted.

"Not a problem," Marg said. "I'll take care of everything. We have your desk set up, as well. Will you be needing us to adjust anything?"

"Thanks, Marg. That's great. Whatever you've set up is fine."

He boarded the plane and immediately went to his desk. But the last thing on his mind was work.

He wanted her. His body was still half-aroused from earlier and sitting so close to her in his sports car had made it worse. He'd driven too fast to burn off some of the adrenaline but she'd simply laughed. The scent of her perfume had surrounded him, egging him on to drive faster. He'd never been one of those men who needed to strut around a woman, but he wanted to with Scarlet. Sure, he could have taken the truck, but the Maserati was a status thing, and she came from a world of immense wealth, so he wanted her to know he wasn't after her money.

Was he after her?

He had told himself and Scarlet that he wanted to get to know her better because she was pregnant with his baby—Scarlet wasn't the kind of woman to lie about that—but another part of him knew that he did want her for himself. And he'd never been comfortable with that sort of longing. He'd grown up one of five kids. Sharing was practically in his DNA. Of course, as an adult he had things that were his, but he always felt greedy when he craved something or, in this case, someone. He wanted Scarlet and it felt so much more intense than just hooking up again.

There was something other than just lust coursing through his veins and he didn't want to acknowledge or examine it. But he was by nature someone who had to figure it out.

"Billie said to give you her regards," Scarlet said as she entered the jet. She bent over to unleash the dog and her honey-blond hair cascaded down over her shoulders. The little dog stood on its back legs and rubbed its face in her hair.

She stood up and their eyes met, and something passed between them. He felt the zing all the way to his groin. No surprise since he'd been turned on since he'd seen her this morning.

"She doesn't like me, so I appreciate you making it seem like she does," he said.

She laughed, throwing her head back. "She thinks she's subtle. Can you believe that?"

"No. She must know she comes across as a bulldog who will protect you at all costs," Alec said.

"Do I need protecting?" she asked, walking toward him. Lulu ran ahead of her and jumped up on one of the seats.

"No," he said, his voice low, gruff and huskier than he wanted it to be. "Not from me."

The thing about addictions, Scarlet thought as she sat next to Alec as the jet took off, was that they were hard to resist. She should have said no, she wouldn't come with him to Seattle. She shouldn't have agreed to be alone with him again until she sorted out what exactly the feelings she had for him were. But honestly, right now, after seeing the way he was watching her and hearing that gravelly tone of voice, all she could think about was how his body had felt against hers and how good it had felt to be straddling him earlier.

For the first time since she'd realized she was pregnant, something made sense. Sex was normal and logical. It didn't have to be complicated. And technically, if she were with Alec, it wasn't breaking her self-imposed rule of hooking only up once with a guy because she'd thought he was Mauricio the last time, right?

She'd started the rule to avoid the situation she was in right now. She couldn't take the chance of falling into the trap of commitment. She'd seen it destroy both her mother and sister.

That makes no sense, even for you. As usual, the voice of her sister nagged her.

Shut up, Tay. I don't want to be logical.

Obviously.

Lulu was curled up and sleeping in her travel crate, which meant there was nothing to distract Scarlet from Alec. He had his legs loosely crossed. When the flight attendants asked if they would like something to eat or drink, he glanced over at her with one eyebrow arched.

"I'm good," she said.

"Me, too. I'll let you know if we need anything," Alec said.

The attendants left to go to the crew quarters and they were alone.

Danger, danger, don't do something stupid.

Tara had been so irresponsible in life that Scarlet knew the voice she often attributed to her sister was simply her own subconscious warning her off. But it comforted her to think her sister might be watching over her.

How dangerous could he be?

You wouldn't be having this conversation with me if you didn't fear something about him.

Fear.

Was that true? Was that what this was?

"Are you comfortable?" he asked. "Do you need a blanket?"

No. She needed him naked and underneath her, so she could feel more in control of everything. He had surprised her and taken the upper hand... Yeah, that was it. She wanted to be on top again. It wasn't anything more than that. She didn't have to fear addiction—this was her first time with Alec. She could have him guilt-free and then go back to figuring out the baby situation.

Yeah, right.

Go away, Tay.

Fine, but don't say I didn't warn you.

"So, tell me more about what you do," she said. "Billie pulled up some information on you, but I'd rather hear your story from you."

"Hmm... I'm not sure where to start," he said. "My job is kind of boring."

She glanced around the plane and remembered his cars and home. "But it pays well. It's nice to know that money can be made by other means than just being Insta-famous."

"Well, when I was in college... Let's just say that I didn't handle being on my own that well. Even though I got straight A's, I drank and partied way too much. I definitely enjoyed those years but when I was a junior and applied for paid internships, no one would even call me back for an interview. I asked one of the HR hiring managers about it and she said I looked good on paper, but the internet told a different story.

"That was a huge wake-up call and I knew that I needed to clean up my online presence. Some of my frat brothers were in the same boat so I wrote some code and created an algorithm that would go in and clean it up. It took a long time, my entire junior year, but once I had it and deployed it, I started getting interviews. I started to sell my services to my frat brothers. Once word got out, I had a lot of customers."

"I could have used you a few years ago," she said with a laugh. "Instead I've just embraced my more scandalous photos and videos and made them my brand."

"That works, too, but sometimes things happen that can really have a negative impact. So I went from helping college kids to helping companies and public figures. I've made a few tweaks along the way to keep up with the technology," he said.

"And it pays well," she said.

"Yeah, it does. Protecting their public image is priceless for some people and businesses. And I provide a service that no one else can," he said. "I did it for Mauricio after the photo of the two of us came out. But Hadley, of course, had already seen it. I monitor all of my family's mentions but it's a soft surveillance. So I just get an alert. I haven't had to use hard surveillance since my brother-in-law, Jose, passed away."

She liked when he talked about his business; she could see his passion for the work he did, and how much he liked it. "Who was Jose and why did you have to monitor him so closely?"

"He was the famous Formula 1 driver Jose Ruiz... Anyway, he wasn't faithful to my sister and there were always lots of photos of him partying with other women. I did it to keep that information private. No one needed to know that he wasn't the perfect husband that he had pretended to be," Alec said. Alec had built his business around a proprietary code that he used to search the internet for any references to Jose and then replaced the salacious stories with a cleaned up reference that focused on his career and not the affairs.

She nodded. He was a protector, she thought. That was another plus if he was going to raise their baby. Add that to the fact that he had a big, incredibly nice family—if her afternoon with them was any indication—a good job and an understanding of the power of reputation.

Now if she could only keep focused on his sterling qualities. But there wasn't anything that could pry the image of his naked chest from her mind. In fact, going back to bed with him, no matter how wrong, was all she could think about.

Talking about work was leveling him out and taking the edge off his desire for Scarlet. It was still there but not as intense as it had been when they'd first boarded the jet. He felt a bit more in control of himself. It had been a long time since he'd discussed the origins of his company with anyone.

In fact, he'd forgotten how out of control he'd been those first two years of college. He had pretty much decided that he'd say yes to everything. It had been fun but he'd been so irresponsible. It was only in his junior year that he'd started to become the man he was today. Someone who understood that following every impulse led to destruction.

But that didn't stop him from wanting Scarlet. He'd like to say he was a twenty-first-century man who could have a conversation with a woman and get to know her without thinking about sex, but he couldn't deny the primal instinct that she brought out in him.

His mom had raised him right and he had a sister so he knew how to treat women. But that didn't mean that there weren't times like this when all he wanted to do was say to hell with being polite and see if she wanted him as much as he wanted her.

"What about you? You said your brand embraced scandal, but I'm not that familiar with your story," he admitted. "Is scandal part of your business plan?" His plan was to keep talking. Then maybe he could get through the flight without making a move on her. If her earlier retreat had sent any signals, it was that she wasn't ready for anything more between them.

"I'm not surprised you don't know my brand. Basically, I have a lifestyle company that is all about embracing your inner... Well, Billie says *bitch* but we don't market it that way. It's called Get-It-Girl. It's just about not apologizing for being yourself. So I have makeup that is very flattering but might also be too bright for some people. But if that's what you like, then you can wear the red lippie and the glitter eye shadow. I also have two clothing lines—one's 'naughty' and the other's 'nice.' It recognizes that everyone is a little bit of both," she said.

"I love that. I think that Penny exemplifies that split every time I see her. To be honest, Benito does, too. It's funny that as children we can embrace these different sides while we learn the limits of how to behave." Penny wasn't strictly his niece but he and his brothers all treated her as if she were. Extended family was the same as family as far as the Velasquezes were concerned.

"That's true. My brand gives you a place to say it's okay to be you," she said. "I have the reality show as well where I just live my social media life and cameras follow me around. I try to show both the partying side and the business side, how you can do what you love and still make a living," she said.

He'd written her off as a party girl heiress when he'd first researched her but he saw now that she was much more than that. "How did you start out?"

He suspected that a lot of this had to stem from her relationship with her father. She'd said he wasn't a good parent to her growing up, and the articles he'd found on the web seemed to support that, even though he knew that the truth was always more complicated than news reports or social media posts.

"I had a really bad screwup when I was eighteen. A sex tape I made went viral and my sister, Tara, said, 'That's it. You're branded with a scarlet letter now.' My response was that my name is Scarlet so maybe it was inevitable and I should embrace it," she said, turning to face him and drawing her legs up on the seat. "Tay said to go for it and I did. I thought if I'm a bad girl in the media, then I could perform in character and control it in a way, even profit from it. You sort of always have to meet that expectation or they go looking for stuff that you don't want to get out."

"I wish I'd met your sister," he said. "She sounds like she was pretty savvy."

"She was, but she was also an idiot. She liked guys that were really bad for her and she never could stay straight."

He reached over to squeeze her hand. "I'm sorry.

I guess it's like you were saying. Everyone is complicated."

"They are. Did you feel that way about your brother-in-law?" she asked. "Everyone is always trying not to speak ill of the dead, but you didn't sugarcoat it with him."

"No, I didn't. I really looked up to him when he and Bianca married but when I saw that first photo… I was so angry. I confronted him, and he said that Bianca knew the score. But I knew my sister. She wasn't the kind of woman who would be happy with a man who cheated on her."

"I don't know many women who would be," Scarlet said.

"I agree," he said. "Jose said that it's in men's natures to be promiscuous."

"Do you agree with him?"

"No, I don't. I think if you find the right woman, she fills that emptiness and you don't have to keep looking," Alec said. "What about you?"

"Hmm… I'm not sure. My dad certainly has never found the One, and Tara didn't, either."

"I didn't ask about them. I want to know if you think you can find it in one man or if you are always looking for something else."

Eight

His question didn't leave much room for anything other than bluntness. "I have no idea."

"Fair enough. I'm just trying to get things straight in my head. I mean a baby isn't going to wait around for the two of us to figure our stuff out, and I do better when I have time to plan," he admitted.

She fidgeted a bit before she realized what she was doing. She needed to stop letting him rattle her, but the truth was she wasn't herself. She hadn't been for a really long time…since Tara's death. But she'd been faking it pretty well until now.

Was it Alejandro who was responsible for the change or was it the baby?

Or both?

She had no idea. She didn't like to do too much introspection because frankly most days she didn't like herself... That was it, wasn't it? The truth of who she'd become: someone who put on a fake show for the media and then played that part until she fell into an exhausted sleep, haunted by her dead sister.

Damn.

She was a bigger mess than she thought.

"I don't know that we're ever going to come up with a plan that will make sense," she admitted.

"Me neither," he said. "I keep trying to wrap my head around having a baby... I'm not going to lie. It's scaring the shit out of me. I mean, I have a nephew but honestly, I don't really spend that much time with kids. Hell, I don't really spend much time with adults who I'm not working with."

She had to laugh at the way he said it. She heard the panic in his voice and it made her feel a little better that he wasn't all cool with everything, either.

"Don't worry, that part I'm good at...not kids but adults," she said, shifting in the large seat and stretching her legs. Lulu was still sleeping in her crate and would probably be content until they landed.

"We should make a list of pros and cons of us becoming parents," he said, pulling his tablet toward him.

She reached over and took it from him, then tucked it behind her on the seat. "No. We're not doing that. We have the rest of this week to spend with each other and we'll learn enough then to figure out what we should do next. Honestly, I thought I'd tell you—I mean, Mauricio—about the baby and then because you, or rather, he was Humanitarian of the Year I'd hand the baby over and he'd raise it. That way it would have a happy, well-adjusted life."

He shook his head. "I really screwed up this time."

"Hey, we both were there that night. You know I wish you'd been honest but no use rehashing that. We'll figure this out."

"I hope so. I don't want to be the reason a kid is messed up," he said.

"Me neither. As I mentioned, my family isn't the greatest when it comes to providing a happy, nurturing home but I still don't want to give up the baby unless we can't figure out a way to raise it."

"You'd give it up?"

"If it meant making sure the child didn't end up like my father or sister, then yes."

She realized that sounded harsh. It was the first time she'd actually said it out loud but in her heart she'd felt that way for a long time. She'd loved Tara more than she'd ever loved anyone on the planet but she'd been so broken, so flawed and it had been so heartbreaking to not be able to help her.

She wouldn't go through that again. She wanted her child to grow up safe and secure…whole. She'd failed Tara and had wanted to save her. Losing Tara had shattered something in her and she was afraid of doing the same thing with her baby.

"We're going to figure this out," he said, the conviction he'd had since the moment he'd found out about her pregnancy...well, after he'd determined that he must be the father.

"That's all I want," she admitted. "I want to get this sorted out before I have to return to New York and start filming my show again."

"When is that?" he asked.

"About three months' time," she said. "I can put them off for a few weeks, but everything hinges on my show. I see increased sales in merchandise when it airs. My company employs about twenty-five people so I can't flake on them."

"No problem. I'm hoping this week will give us both the answers we want. I know I want to get to know you better and I hope you'll see that I'm not as craven as I might have seemed at first when I lied about who I was."

"I'm already seeing it," she said. No use hiding the truth from him. Billie always said she had no filter, which also meant she had no walls up to protect herself. But honestly she couldn't stand fake emotion in her real life. She spent so much time projecting an image to the world via her media channels that when she had downtime she had to be real.

"Good," he said. "I am, too. I had no idea how honest you would be about everything. I sort of expected you to think about how it would affect your follows and stuff like that."

She shook her head and shifted away from him. "I'm not like that. I mean I do have to be aware of how I look and the image I present but I'm not shallow."

"I know. That's what I was trying to say. I'm really good at putting my foot in it and saying the wrong things, but believe me, my intent is never to be an ass."

She had to smile at that. She noticed he used self-deprecation a lot to divert tension. She wasn't sure if it was sincere or if that was his way of pushing any blame away from himself. For now, she was going to take it at face value but it was something for her to watch.

"Fair enough," she said. "So what do you usually do during the flight?"

"Work," he said.

"Work?"

"Yeah," he said. "Or work out. I have a treadmill in the bedroom."

She shook her head. He was surprising. She hadn't pegged him for a workaholic but as she looked around the aircraft she could see it was set up as an office. She also noticed a client entertainment area.

"Well… What are we going to do?"

"Whatever you want," he said.

Whatever she wanted… Now that was dangerous invitation.

* * *

He hadn't expected to find himself sitting across his conference table from her with a deck of cards between them. But then everything about Scarlet was unexpected so maybe he should stop trying to anticipate what she'd do.

He, his brothers and their friends had a monthly poker game in Cole's Hill and he was pretty good at reading them. They'd played together since high school when they'd thought they were cooler than they actually had been. But Scarlet was completely different. It was harder for him to find her tells. And not just because she had a pretty good poker face, but because she distracted him.

She'd braided her long blond hair, but tendrils had escaped, with one of them brushing against the side of her face. She kept reaching up and tucking the strand behind her ear, which fascinated him. He'd seen his sister, Bianca, do the same thing, but it had never seemed as interesting as when Scarlet did it.

"I'll raise you a protein bar and two Hershey's Kisses," she said, pushing the snacks toward the middle of the table.

He arched one eyebrow at her. "That's a pretty steep bet."

"It is… Though I have heard that you should never wager anything you don't want to lose, so if you really want to keep your protein bar you should fold."

He shook his head. "No way. I'm sort of an all-in kind of guy."

"Are you?" she asked. "You seem like an I-don't-place-a-bet-unless-I'm-going-to-win kind of guy."

"Possibly," he said with a shrug. "In life, definitely, but when it comes to cards I have a different set of rules."

She nodded. "You're all about the rules, aren't you?"

He didn't think she meant that as a good thing and thought maybe he should hedge his answer. But when she'd been brutally honest about her family, he'd decided to do the same with her. Keep it real instead of trying to protect himself from letting her see too much of who he was. "I know it makes me sound like an old fart, but I am about the rules. Life is just so much easier when we all know what to expect."

"Why break them the night of the gala, then? And who called you an old fart?" she asked, laughing. "I mean I haven't exactly seen that side of you. At the gala you were definitely not acting like a stick-in-the-mud."

"My brothers and Bianca call me that. But that's just because they usually don't follow the rules and end up in trouble. The night of the gala... I don't know, I guess I just felt like I could let go because no one knew it was me. It gave me a chance to just let my guard down. And I imitated Alec the night of the gala because he needed me. I can't turn down family."

"That's sweet. I liked you at the gala," she said.

"You did?" he asked, leaning across the table. He wanted her so badly that every inhalation was almost painful. He could smell her perfume. His senses were overwhelmed with everything that was Scarlet. He struggled to keep his eyes off the curves of her body and that damned strand of hair she kept tucking behind her ear. He knew if he shifted his legs under the table he'd brush against her; he had done it twice already and had the feeling she'd catch on to what he was doing if he did it again.

He was trying but it was hard. He was hard, and he wanted nothing more than to forget all the rules that he applied to his life to keep it orderly, sweep her into his arms and carry her into the bedroom at the back of the plane.

"I did," she said.

He groaned.

"What?"

"You're not making this easy."

"Making what easy?"

"Just sticking to my own tips for not screwing things up with you any further than I already have," he said.

She laughed again and it made him smile. The sound was so genuine and full of joy that he couldn't help himself. Which only underscored how important it was for him to stick to his own regulations where she was concerned.

"I have to admit I like that," she said.

"You do?"

"Yes. You aren't what I expected, Alec, and I like it better when I know I'm not the only one struggling to figure things out."

That wasn't all he was struggling with. "My brothers would give me tons of shit if they ever heard about this."

"Why?"

"Because that's how brothers are," he said.

"And… You're the goody-goody in the Velasquez family, aren't you?"

"I guess. I mean, I'm not a nerdy rule follower. I just like to stay within safe limits," he said, then groaned again as he realized exactly how that sounded. "Okay, so I am a goody-goody. But I've been burned when I just let go of all my limits and I realized that I have to know which lines I can't cross."

"Fair enough," she said. "So, back to the game. Are you going to call?"

Call? No. He wanted more than her protein bar and chocolate. He wanted kisses, but real kisses. He wanted the stakes to be higher and he knew the risk. He could move too fast and push her away. But as Mo would say, you have to take a chance if you ever want the big prize.

And he wanted her…badly.

"I'm going to raise," he said at last.

"You are?"

"Yes," he said, pushing the requisite ante into the center of the table. "I call and raise you one kiss."

"A kiss? I have two in there," she said.

"No, I mean a real one. A bodies-pressed-together, mouths-fused, passion-filled kiss."

"Oh," she said, a slight flush spreading up her neck to her cheeks. "Very well, I call."

He stretched his legs, and the fabric of his trousers brushed against her. She shifted so that her calves rested against his as he slowly laid his cards on the table. She glanced at the pair of tens with an ace high that he'd revealed and then back at her own hand.

She had two pairs so that beat him. She had always been a believer that she shouldn't wager anything she didn't want to lose, and frankly, she had been craving Alec since the moment they'd been alone in the barn at the polo match. Nothing had changed since then.

Of course, she'd retreated, but that was because he was different. The type of guy she normally attracted would have pushed for a kiss or more until she either gave in or shoved him out of her life. But Alec was subtle and funny. He was carefully feeling his way along trying to get to know her better and maybe let her see the real man.

She fanned her cards out on the table and then crossed her arms under her breasts as she leaned back in the large leather chair. "Read 'em and weep."

He chewed his lower lip between his teeth and gave her a steely-eyed look. "I see I'm going to have to reevaluate you. I was sure you were bluffing."

"I wasn't," she said.

"Obviously. But you played it so cool I couldn't tell. Interesting. I think that means you must spend a lot of time hiding who you really are," he said.

"Dude, I said you could have a kiss, not psycho-analyze me."

He leaned across the table, reaching out to tuck a strand of her hair behind her ear. "Sorry. It's just that I haven't wanted a woman the way I want you in a long time. I'm trying to give myself a bit of time to gain some control."

Again she was struck by how he seemed to have no barriers when it came to her. She wanted to believe in him but as he'd noted a minute ago, experience had taught her that what she really needed to do was to keep her true self hidden. It was just better for her. There had been only one person she'd ever felt comfortable letting her guard down around and that had been Tara.

And she was still trying to recover from the pain of losing her the way that she had. She really didn't want to go down that dark and emotional path so she leaned forward, elbows on the table, putting her hands on his wrists. "So about the kiss I've won in this hand."

"What about it?" he asked.

"I'm trying to decide if I should take my prize and walk or keep it in the ante and see if I can win again."

He took her left hand in his, his thumb stroking her palm and sending shivers of sensation up her arm, making her breasts feel heavy.

"Up to you," he said. "You call the shots."

As if. She realized that was cynical but she'd been in too many situations like this to believe that one person called all the shots. Sex was intimate and involved so much more than power in her experience.

"I see you don't believe me," he said. "I'm not playing around with you, Scarlet. I know I lied to you the first night we met but you're pregnant with my baby. I want you more than I want my next breath and that makes me feel dangerous…out of control. I don't want to be that way. Not when so much is at stake."

Again he disarmed her with the truth. His earnestness made her want to believe him yet every experience in her life had shown her that when she most wanted to trust in another person, they let her down. And he was right: the stakes here were high. They both wanted to make sure they didn't add another screwed-up being to the planet. Both of them wanted better for the baby she was carrying.

And maybe that was enough.

Of course it is. Tara's voice sounded in her head. *Stop dithering and kiss the man. It's what you want.*

It was what she wanted so she pushed away from the table and went around to his side. She put her hands on the arm of his chair and spun it so he faced her. Then she sat down on his lap, sitting sideways so that her legs hung over the armrest and she could see his face. One of his arms came around her waist and the other one just hovered in the air over her body, not touching her.

She lifted her hand to his face, touched the light stubble on his jaw and looked into his dark brown eyes, searching for something in his gaze but not really knowing what it was. She sighed inside and realized there were no guarantees. This could be nothing more than a nice way to spend the flight or it could be the most dangerous decision she ever made.

But she wasn't someone who cowered. And Tara's voice in her head had reminded her of that.

She rubbed her thumb over his full lower lip and his mouth parted, his breath coming out in a sudden gasp. She felt him harden under her hips. She leaned in closer, taking her time because now that she'd made up her mind, there was no rush. Regardless of the outcome, she wanted and intended to make this last.

Their eyes met and she felt something shift and settle deep inside her. At least they had this one thing that made sense between them. The rest of their lives were crazy right now, but this, she thought as she leaned in and brushed her lips over his, made perfect sense.

Nine

His hands were shaking; it was all he could do to keep himself under control. But she was on his lap, her mouth so close to his that he felt each exhalation of her breath against his lips, and it served to fan the flames that were edging ever more untamable.

He put his hand on her shoulder, forcing himself to keep his touch light and not caress her skin. But the neckline of her sweater was wide, and he had brushed her naked skin as his fingers came to rest there. He wanted to stroke and caress her more, but he had promised her she was in control. That he'd settle for whatever she wanted to give him.

But he knew deep in his soul that he wanted it all.

He wanted every damned thing she had to give. Her lips brushed his and sensation went through him, making his blood run heavier in his veins and hardening his cock. He shifted underneath her to try to make himself more comfortable within the tight confines of his pants.

She smiled against his mouth as she kept the kiss light. Just a mere pressing of her lips against his. Then she moved her head slightly and their lips rubbed together more intimately. The hair on the back of his neck stood up and a sensual shiver went down his spine. He moved his hand from her collarbone to the back of her neck, cupping it as he turned his head slightly and deepened the kiss.

She tasted better than he remembered... And given that it hadn't been that long since he'd last kissed her, he was surprised. Surely, she hadn't become more addictive in those few hours since their kiss. But it seemed she had. His hand tangled in her braid as he cupped the back of her head and leaned up to take her mouth more deeply. He heard the tiny moan from deep in her throat and he answered in kind.

He rubbed his hand down her back, taking his time so that he felt each curve of her spine. Then he shifted his head back to look up at her as he put both hands on her waist and lifted her until she could straddle his lap.

She clutched his shoulders and settled her thighs

on either side of his hips. He inhaled deeply, smelled the slight hint of roses and something spicier, a more sensual scent that he remembered from the night of the gala.

He slipped his hands under the hem of her sweater and held her against him as he looked up at her. She smiled, just the tiniest lift of one side of her mouth, before she leaned down, resting her forehead against his. Then he felt the brush of her tongue against his lips.

He groaned, and got even harder. He wasn't going to be able to live up to his word and take just a kiss if she kept this up. Already he wanted more. He wanted her leggings off and her naked body pressed against him.

He wanted this sweater gone and them both naked with him buried deep inside her. But he knew that he had to temper that desire. Had to make this last. He'd given his word and if he didn't live up to it, she'd always remember.

He slipped one hand up her back and used the other on her waist to draw her even closer to him, until their groins were pressed together. She rocked her hips against him and he tore his mouth from hers, tipping his head back as exquisite sensation shot through him.

She shifted farther forward, grasping at his sides, and he held one of her arms lightly in his hand as he deepened the kiss. Their tongues tangled as he rubbed his hand up and down her arm, pulling the edge of her sweater down so that her collarbone was exposed. He touched her there, caressing her; her skin was softer than he remembered.

He pulled his mouth from hers, dropping nibbling kisses down the column of her throat and then sucking lightly on the pulse that beat under her skin. She shivered in his arms as he moved his mouth along the line of her collarbone to her shoulder. She put one hand on the back of his head, her fingers burrowing into his hair and holding him against her. He breathed deeply, the scent of her more potent now that he held her in his arms.

He closed his eyes, reaching deep inside for his control, but it was slipping so quickly through his grasp. The hand he had on the small of her back slipped down to cup her butt, rubbing over the spandex fabric of her leggings and drawing her ever closer to him. She shifted, still holding his head against her as she arched her back and rubbed her center over him. They both groaned out loud and he turned his head, using his nose to push the collar of her sweater down farther, kissing his way down her chest following the line of her bra. The straps were lacy, contrasting with the smoothness of her skin. He moved lower, still following the seams of her lingerie, tasting the sweetness that was Scarlet. He knew that he wasn't going to be able to take it slow for much longer, yet at the same time he wanted this to last. Wanted to keep her in his arms for as long as he could.

He buried his face between her breasts. His hand was on her butt urging her closer to him and her hands were in his hair, one fingernail tracing the shape of his ear. When the plane hit turbulence and they were jolted, he wrapped his arms around her, holding her close to him until the aircraft leveled out.

Her heart raced from lust, and the dipping of the plane. She should get off his lap, but she'd decided she wasn't doing that. This wasn't an unhealthy addiction. This was something natural between the two of them and she wasn't going to deny herself. Also, she felt like she needed to treat him as she would any other guy. How else could she judge this situation that was so far out of her experience?

"Are you okay?" he asked.

His voice was raspy, scraping over her already aroused senses and confirming her desire to have him. Now.

"Yes. That was jarring, though," she said.

He reached around her and pressed a button in the arm of his chair.

"Yes, sir?"

"Will we be encountering any more turbulence?" Alec asked.

"No, sir, we haven't heard reports of it. That was

an anomaly and we should be fine," the pilot answered.

"Great. Thank you."

"No problem. Do you need anything?"

"We're fine and do not wish to be disturbed," he said.

"Yes, sir."

He put his hands on her waist over her sweater and looked up at her with a very serious look on his face.

"Do you want to stop?" he asked.

She felt his erection still pressing against her. His skin was flushed, his pupils dilated, and his voice still betrayed his lust.

"No. Do you?"

"I don't, but I'd never want you to feel pressured," he said.

"I don't," she returned. "Do you?"

He shook his head, slipping his hands under her sweater, cupping her butt and rubbing it. "What do you think?"

He pulled her forward, thrusting his hips up so that her center rubbed over the ridge of his cock. She let her head fall back at the exquisiteness of the feeling that washed over her.

"I think we should stop talking," she said, putting one hand on the back of his head as she brought her mouth down hard on his.

He groaned as his hands moved up to the waistband of her leggings. He pushed beneath it to touch the naked skin of her back, his fingers feathering downward until he was cupping her butt, this time without any fabric separating them. He ran his finger along the bottom of her butt cheek and lifted her higher against him.

He pulled his mouth from hers, kissing her in the center of her chest, slightly to the right of her heart. He used his other hand to tug at the hem of her sweater and pulled it up over her head. She moved her arms to help him remove it.

He kept stroking her backside as his gaze moved over her chest. He drew his finger down her body from her neck to the V created by her bra and then up the other side of her body. She felt the goose pimples rise and her nipples tighten as he continued to trace her skin. She wanted more of his touch and yet enjoyed the feel of just his fingertips on her skin.

"You have the smoothest skin I've ever touched," he admitted, licking his way down her body. "It's one of the things I couldn't forget about you after our night together. I thought I'd imagined how soft you were…"

His words were whispered against her skin as he moved his mouth down her neck. She shifted around, her braid coming forward to brush over her shoulder, the end of it brushing against his nose.

She'd always been the girl to take a risk but this time, with Alec, it felt different. The first time they'd been together hadn't been all that risky or bold. Not really. It had just been a bit of fun with a guy she thought she'd never see again.

This time it was different. She was consciously choosing to be with a man she was connected to through this baby, a situation that she still couldn't really wrap her head around.

He reached up to tug off the elastic that held her braid in place and dropped it on the table next to them. He pulled the plait apart and then ran both hands through the long strands of her hair, drawing it forward until the ends draped over her shoulders. Her hair was long enough that it reached the top of her breasts. He reached behind her, undoing her bra, and then she shrugged it off, setting it on the table next to them.

He continued to run his hands through her hair. "You smell like spring, fresh and flowery. After our night together, I couldn't get your scent out of my mind. I made my housekeeper crazy trying to figure out the smell by ordering different bouquets of flowers."

"Did you figure it out?" she asked as he leaned forward and brought a strand of her hair to his nose.

"No."

"It's a mix of strawberries, magnolias and freesia. Sounds like it shouldn't work but for some reason it does," she said with a laugh, realizing that she was nervous. She was talking to him during sex and that made it more intimate than their one-night stand. They hadn't talked, just kissed and touched and made love.

But this was different. It was deliberate. And that both excited her and scared her.

He felt a pulse of desire between his legs and realized he couldn't take his time. He was too hot for Scarlet but then had been since the beginning.

He tongued her nipple, then scraped his teeth gently over it. She arched again, grinding her hips against his. He tugged at the waistband of her leggings and she shifted position, drawing them down her legs and standing up to take them off. She stood next to his chair totally naked and he couldn't think. Couldn't breathe. Couldn't do anything except lift her into his arms and carry her to the bedroom at the back of the jet.

He opened the door with one hand and then kicked it closed behind him as he entered the room. He set her on her feet next to the bed, and she reached for the buttons on his shirt, slowly undoing them and distracting him from the urgency of getting his pants off.

The red haze that had fallen over him lifted as he slowly wrested control back. He could do this. Still be cool and not fall on her like a man enflamed with lust and passion…maybe.

He kicked off his loafers and shoved his jeans and

underwear down his legs as she pushed his shirt off his shoulders. As soon as he was naked, he felt better. This was how they should both be.

She touched his chest; her fingers were slightly cold as she drew them over his pectorals. She ran her nail around the edge of the muscles and then slowly back up to his neck. Her touch sent shivers down his body and he felt like he was on the verge of losing control once again. He truly wasn't sure how much longer he was going to be able to let her touch him.

He wanted to draw this out so it felt like making love and not a hurried coupling. They'd had sex twice the night of the gala and he'd still woken up hungry for her again. Would he ever be able to satisfy that hunger?

She was so pretty and feminine. He traced her curves from her shoulder down to her hips, trying to be cool like he wasn't dying to caress her, to taste her intimately. But he knew he was.

He slowly moved his fingers up her thigh to her hip bone and then down to the cradle of her womanhood. He ran his fingers along the neatly trimmed pubic hair and then lower as she scored his chest with her nails.

She rocked her hips forward as he touched her, tapping lightly on her, and she moaned. As she was stroking him, he couldn't help but rub the length of himself against her. She wrapped her arms around his shoulders and he put his arm behind her as he tipped her back onto the bed, coming down over her.

She arched her back as he caught her nipple in his mouth and suckled it. At the same time, he palmed her body and thrust the tip of one finger inside her, drawing out the wet tip, bringing it to his mouth and licking it.

He sat back on his knees and looked down at her. Their eyes met, and he knew that he was never going to be the same after this.

"I'd forgotten how good you are."

He leaned down to taste her again, used his tongue to seek out the tiny bud between her legs, flicking it again and again as her hands held his head to her, her hips lifting into each flick of his tongue. Her legs tightened around him as he continued to eat her.

She clasped him tightly to her as her hips rose frantically, her legs scissoring around him. Then she called out his name and felt her orgasm roll through her body.

Her body was still buzzing and pulsing from her climax. It was nice but she needed Alec inside her.

She pulled him up and over her, lifting her torso so she could find his mouth and take it in a deep kiss. She took in the salty taste of her own passion on his tongue, as she felt him enter her. She held on to his broad shoulders and arched her back, pushing up against him to drive him deeper.

He groaned and called her name as he pulled back

and then thrust into her, taking her even deeper than he had before. He was big and solid and filled her completely. She let her head fall back as he drove himself into her again and again. She felt the tingling in her body, and each time he thrust into her she craved more.

Twisting his hand in her hair, he held her head so her neck was exposed and dropped a light bite against her there. It sent off a chain reaction inside her, and her second orgasm took her by surprise.

She clutched him to her as she rode her orgasm, and he lowered his head, taking one of her nipples into his mouth and suckling her. His hips were moving faster and faster until she heard him grunt as he emptied himself inside her. He kept thrusting until he was completely empty and then rolled to his side, taking her with him. He tucked her up against him and stroked her back.

She refused to let herself think about anything other than this moment. She was in the arms of a man whom she'd slept with before. She was going to have a relationship with him whether she wanted one or not, and instead of it making her want to get up and run away, she curled closer to him. He fumbled around for the edge of the comforter and drew it over her.

"Are you okay?" he asked.

"I'm good," she said.

He kissed her forehead and held her lightly in his arms.

Something had changed inside her and she pretended it hadn't.

Ten

The week in Seattle had cemented a bond between her and Alec that had been unexpected. In the last six weeks or so since they'd returned, she had balanced between Cole's Hill and trying to get to know Alec and his family and her commitments in New York. She was still having some morning sickness but it had started to settle down. She'd tried to make sure she was in Cole's Hill for the "book club" on Friday nights with Hadley and Helena and their friends. She'd taken Lulu for walks around the neighborhood and enjoyed how quiet it was. A part of her sort of liked it here.

Now she was sitting by his pool under the shade

of an umbrella on a lazy Saturday afternoon. Lulu was sleeping in the sun on a cushion that Alec had set up on the patio close to a bowl of water. Music was already blaring from the speakers. She noticed that Alec liked Drake and Childish Gambino but occasionally something from Pitbull would pop up.

His family was coming over later for a cookout and tomorrow they were going to a baby shower for his sister, Bianca.

Lying on the sun lounger with her shades on, she felt like she could be a woman who would fit in here. Her baby was growing, and she had a doctor's appointment next week in Cole's Hill just to make sure things were still on track. She'd flown her doctor in from New York for her last monthly checkup, but Alec had suggested she see someone local just to be on record as a patient.

She stretched her legs out and placed her hand on her abdomen. The baby wasn't big enough for her to feel it move yet, but she knew it was in there.

Alec's shadow covered her, and she glanced up. "Do you mind if I sit down here?"

She shifted her legs to give him room to sit next to her on the chair. He handed her the bowl of strawberries that he'd gone to get for her. To be honest, Alec spoiled her and she liked it. All she had to do was mention she was hungry or that the strawberries they'd picked up at the market looked good and he was off making her a bowl.

He put his hand on her thigh and that familiar buzz of desire and lust started humming through her body. He caressed her inner thigh and then she noticed him watching her.

"What is it?" she asked. "Thanks for the strawberries by the way."

"No problem. Do you mind if I touch your stomach?" he asked. "It's hard to believe our child is in there."

She set the bowl aside and took his hand in hers, placing it on her stomach. She had a slight pooch there now, but really it wasn't easy to tell from just looking at her that she was pregnant. Alec, being the superefficient man he was, had researched the different stages of pregnancy and had sent her a pdf containing all the information. It had made her smile when she'd received the text.

Other men might send flowers or expensive gifts, but Alec Velasquez was too practical for that.

"Yes, it is. Now that the morning sickness is over, I'm not really that affected by the child…except for these," she said, gesturing to her boobs, which were already half a cup size larger than usual.

"I noticed that," he admitted.

"Given that you couldn't keep your hands off me last night, I'm not surprised," she said with a smile. "I have a doctor's appointment this week. Do you want to come with me?"

Each step in her pregnancy, she was starting to

see how good Alec was at adapting to the situation. There were moments that had clearly taken him by surprise but there were also many that seemed to show he was in his element.

"I'd like that. Do you have the details?"

"I'll text them to you later," she said.

He leaned over and kissed her before standing up and moving back to his own chair. "Are you okay?"

"I don't know. I'm still trying to adjust to you being pregnant and I'm not sure I'm doing the right thing. I mean I want you but I'm not sure that I should… I mean you're pregnant."

"Dude, I was pregnant on the jet and in Seattle and last night and that didn't stop you," she said.

"Maybe it should have," he said. "I mean pretty much we're still strangers and you're having my baby… which makes me think of my *abuela*'s favorite show, *I Love Lucy*, and that episode where Ricky sings… I'm losing it. I don't know how to act anymore. I mean I can't be the guy I was because I'm going to be a dad. I don't know if I'm ready."

She swung her legs to the side of the chair and leaned forward to touch his hand. "Hey. I'm not ready. That pdf you sent said that the nine months of pregnancy are supposed to help you prepare for the child."

"I don't know if nine months is going to be enough," he admitted.

"Me, either," she said. It was the first time they'd

really talked about the baby. She felt like that was partially her fault because she'd been trying to make things between herself and Alec just feel normal instead of…like this. "I've never had a relationship with a guy before that's lasted this long."

"We've barely been seeing each other six weeks," he said.

"I know. It's just the way I normally am. I don't know how to do this," she admitted.

"Well, the sex seems to be good between us," he said, smiling and tangling their fingers together.

"It does… But is that all there is to a relationship?" she asked, moving over to sit on his lap. He wrapped his arms around her waist as she cupped his jaw.

"No. We also have to get to know things about each other," he said.

"Like what?"

"Well, I know you like strawberries," he said.

"And you like Lone Star beer," she said.

"We should probably learn a few more things about each other before we call it a relationship," he joked.

"You like Drake…a lot."

"I do," he admitted. "What about you?"

"Well, of course I like Siobahn's songs but my comfort listen is jazz standards from the thirties and forties."

"What? The brand influencer likes old-timey music?" he teased.

"I do," she admitted. "And you're the only one who knows."

"I'm honored," he said.

"You should be," she said, stretching up to kiss him as she put her arms around his shoulders. She pressed herself against his naked chest and in this moment she didn't let herself worry over what she was going to do when the nine months were up and her baby was here. Instead she just enjoyed the afternoon in the sun with her lover.

Alec shifted on the sun lounger made for two so that they were lying side by side and he was cuddling her from behind. Their bodies fit together perfectly, her curves settling against his angles. His hand was warm on her hip as he caressed her. His head rested on her shoulder as he continued to ask her questions about things she liked and didn't like.

This was like nothing she'd ever experienced before and a part of her wished that it wasn't happening. She had that weird feeling again. It was warm and almost comforting. She associated it with Alec but she couldn't say for sure what it was. She thought she might be starting to care for him.

She didn't want that.

Sex was one thing. But if she let herself start caring... She admitted to herself she was afraid that she might not be able to control herself with Alec if she cared. She was trying to get to know him without allowing herself to need him. She couldn't need him except as a father for her baby. She knew that she wasn't facing the fact that she was going to have make a decision about the baby's future and she was starting to care for Alec. But she couldn't allow herself to feel anything other than lust for him.

She turned in his arms. His hands stayed at her waist and when she faced him, seeing the stubble on his jaw and the intensity of his gaze, she knew that lust was definitely a big draw for both of them.

He leaned down to kiss her and she caught his bottom lip between her teeth, sucking on it. Then he shifted his head and his mouth was on hers, his lips firm as he slowly kissed her. He moved his head back and forth, until her lips parted and she felt the exhalation of his breath into her mouth. He tasted of lime and tequila and something that she associated only with Alec. She opened her mouth to invite him deeper.

She shivered as she wrapped her arms around him and draped one thigh over his hips, trying to get closer to him. The taste of him always made her hungry for more.

"I'm having another craving," she whispered against his jaw.

"What is it for?" he asked, his hands moving up and down her body.

"You," she admitted.

She squeezed his shoulders, then moved her hands

up his neck to cup the back of his head. His hair was thick and silky under her fingers. God, she wanted him. And it was okay to admit it because sex was safe. Not like hearing him talk about her having his baby. This made sense. This she understood.

He caressed her back, his fingers tracing a delicate pattern down her spine. Then he pushed one of his hands beneath her bikini bottom to cup her naked flesh. She rubbed her backside against his hand, liking the feel of it.

He ran his other hand up the curve of her waist and around to her chest. She shifted back and their eyes met as he moved his hand up to her breasts, which were almost too big for her bikini top now that her pregnancy was advancing. He traced his finger around the triangles of fabric, then slowly dipped one under it to brush over her already aroused nipple.

Delicate tremors went through her entire body. He kept one hand on her butt and one fingertip idly circling her nipple. She shifted in his arms, trying to get closer to him.

He lowered his head, his lips gliding down the column of her neck. Then she felt his teeth on the bikini tie at the back of her neck. He twisted his head and the bow came undone, then he caught one strap between his lips and drew it forward until one of her breasts was exposed…the one he wasn't caressing with his finger.

"Oh, hello," he said, lowering his head and circling that nipple with his tongue. Her head fell back, and she clutched at his shoulders as he took her into his mouth and sucked eagerly. Every nerve in her body seemed to constrict with desire and her center was damp and aching for him.

He shifted her suddenly so that she was lying on her back underneath him as he knelt over her. His mouth continued to drive her mad and all she was aware of was the delicious feelings he was pulling from her.

His muscled thigh pushed between her legs, nudging them apart, and she felt the ridge of his erection rubbing against her. She lifted her hips, moving her body under his until he rubbed her in just the right spot.

She ran her hands down his back, reaching the point in the small of his back that made his hips jerk forward against him. He eased down her body, kissing her from her midriff down to her belly button. He eased even lower, nibbling at the skin of her belly where he'd touched her earlier.

He kissed her there and whispered something against her stomach that she couldn't hear before he dipped his tongue into the indentation left by her belly button. She felt an answering pulse between her legs. She gyrated underneath him and he pushed back, his erection thrusting against her leg.

His mouth went lower on her, his hands roaming to the waistband of her bikini bottoms and slowly drawing them down to her thighs. She wanted to push them lower, but she felt his moist breath against her stomach and then the scratchiness of his stubble as he rubbed his jaw against her.

"Lift up," he said.

She planted her feet on the sun lounger and did as he asked. He shoved her bikini bottoms the rest of the way down her legs. Their eyes met and he held her gaze as he put his hand on her feminine center. Her skin felt too sensitive and her blood felt like it was boiling in her veins. She was on fire for him. She had never expected to still want him just as badly over so much time. She thought that their lovemaking wouldn't be as intense after all these weeks.

She was wrong.

He spoke against her skin, telling her what he was going to do to her, how much he loved the feel of her naked body under his. Then he lowered his head again, his chin brushing her center as he twisted his head back and forth. The movement put pressure on her, causing her clit to swell and become more sensitive.

He parted her using both of his hands and she felt the brush of the cold air against her most intimate flesh. Then he warmed her with his mouth, breathing over her. She squirmed against him hungrily.

She felt the rasp of his teeth against her and everything inside her clenched, almost making her come.

But Alec lifted his head at the last minute, leaving her yearning for more.

"I want to make this last," he admitted.

She put her hands on the back of his head and directed him back to her clit. "Later we can make it last. I need you now."

She felt one of his hands go lower, tracing her opening. Those large knowing hands of his made her push up against him with need. Everything in her body was on the edge. He pushed his finger—just the tip—inside her and she felt the first ripples of her orgasm rushing through her. He pulled back, lifting his head to watch her as she undulated beneath him.

"Alec…"

"Yes?" he asked.

"I need you inside me."

"Perfect. That's what I need, too," he said, lowering his body over hers so the warm flesh of his chest rubbed against her breasts. Then his thigh was between her legs brushing against her engorged flesh, and she wanted to scream as everything in her tightened just a little bit more.

"Alec!"

She twisted underneath him, clawing at his shoulders as he thrust up and inside her. He drove into her again and again until she was crying out his name, and he shouted hers against her shoulder. They came long and hard and then afterward he held her in his arms, shifting to his side to hold her. She looked up at him.

And that funny feeling was back, even more intense this time. *Oh, God.* She wasn't sure she was ready to admit that she liked him this much.

"I guess we know something else about each other."

"What's that?" he asked, tucking a strand of hair behind her ear.

"We both don't have a problem getting naked in the great outdoors."

He started laughing and then shook his head. "Very true."

Eleven

The longer Scarlet stayed in Cole's Hill, the deeper the bond grew between her and Alex. His family and friends had accepted her into their circle and she was feeling for the first time in her life that it might be okay to let her guard down with more than just a select few people.

A couple of hours in, Bianca's baby shower was in full swing. All of the Velasquez brothers were in attendance, which was a big deal since Inigo had come fresh from a Formula 1 race to make it. Benito was proudly wearing a shirt that said I'm the Big Brother and because he was close with Nate and Kinley's daughter, Penny, Penny had a shirt that said "I'm the

Big Cousin." The two of them were thick as thieves and it made Scarlet smile to see the way Alec's entire family embraced Bianca's baby.

Alec had been locked away in the den for several hours discussing something with Inigo, but she hadn't missed him. She was seated on the couch with Helena, Hadley and Kinley, and honestly, she'd never had more fun.

She'd sent Billie back to New York to get ready for the launch of her newest lifestyle box, a quarterly subscription that included trendy products, and Siobahn was still lying low at the house that Scarlet had rented. She'd started writing music again and Scarlet felt her friend was finally moving on from the heartbreak that had been dominating her life for so long.

Being surrounded by so much domestic bliss today brought her to an idea she'd been toying with for a while. She'd never really been able to crack the market of women who were older and maybe settling down. Her audience members were young and single and pretty much interested in working hard and partying hard. But spending time with Helena and Kinley made her think of maybe curating a wedding/bride subscription box. As the demographic of her audience was maturing, this might be a logical next step.

"Are you two available tomorrow to discuss a new project I'm working on?" Scarlet said. "I'm sort of known for my monthly lifestyle boxes and I'd love to do one with a wedding or bridal theme. Kinley, maybe I can partner with Jaqs if you think she'd be interested and include some exclusive content. Helena, as a bride-to-be, it'd be great to get your input on what to include."

"I love this idea," Kinley said. "I'll text Jaqs after the party. She's always looking to expand into new markets. We've been working on an exclusive tiara collection with Pippa and House of Hamilton. Maybe we could bring her into this as well with some bridesmaids' gifts."

"Sweet," Scarlet said.

"I'm happy to help but honestly the things I'm interested in might be out of step with most brides. Like I've been majorly stressed by things that aren't necessarily planning related," Helena said.

"Hmm… Maybe we could include some tips from meditation experts, too. So it wouldn't just be actual wedding products but wellness items, too. So will tomorrow work for you two to discuss the details?"

Kinley nodded, and Helena pulled out her smartphone, glanced at her calendar and then back at the two of them. "I could do early afternoon, but I have to combine it with lunch. Maybe around one or one thirty."

"That's fine with me," Scarlet said.

"I'm good with that, as well. Tomorrow I'm working on Helena's wedding, so I can move around a few things," Hadley said.

"Mom won't like that," Helena warned.

"Your mom's going to Vegas to meet with Jaqs. She and Jaqs have become closer after their blowup," Kinley interjected.

Alec knew there had to be more to the story and she was interested in hearing it, but the main festivities of the baby shower were starting. She realized she'd never been to a party like this one. It was multigenerational, and almost everyone at the party had known each other for most of their lives. There was a lot of joking and reminiscing.

She looked over at Mr. Velasquez and tried to imagine her father ever attending a baby shower but frankly couldn't. He wanted nothing to do with babies because they'd make him seem older or settled.

She already knew he wasn't going to be a doting grandfather… Why would he be? He hadn't exactly embraced fatherhood.

Just then Alec entered the room holding a plate of food from the buffet and a glass of sparkling water. He came over and handed them to her. "Figured you'd be getting hungry."

"Thank you," she said, taking the plate and drink from him. They'd discovered while she was in Seattle that if she ate something every hour she didn't get sick.

"Looks like someone has broken Alec," Mauricio said as he joined them.

"Mo, he's not a horse," Hadley said.

"What is he?"

"A gentleman… In fact, you could take lessons from your twin. I don't think you've ever brought me a plate of food."

"I give you other things," Mo said, drawing his fiancée into his arms and kissing her, much to the delight of everyone in the room.

Helena got up and Alec took her spot next to Scarlet. "I like your family," she said to him.

"Me, too. They are a bit of a pain sometimes because everyone feels like they know best but at the end of the day they'll always be there for me," he said, stretching his arm along the back of the sofa and wrapping it around her shoulder.

Alec was turning out to be an even better man than she'd expected to find, and his family would be exactly what her child needed. She felt better and better about the prospects for her baby, and that made her decision easier. She knew that if things didn't work out in her relationship with Alec—and frankly, she wasn't expecting them to, because she'd never been able to make one last more than six months—at least her child would still have a decent family to raise it.

Sometimes she started to think that they might be able to be a couple and raise the baby together. But there were times when she woke up sweating and scared thinking about the possibility that the baby would grow up and be in the place Tara had been toward the end of her life She had failed her sister and she didn't want to fail her child.

Helena wasn't too sure if she should bring up Scarlet's request to Malcolm, but she wasn't hiding anything from him. They were doing pretty well but she had been careful not to do anything that would rock the boat. She knew that wasn't a healthy way to treat him but she'd been afraid of doing something that would drive him back to gambling. So as soon as he got home from work after picking up takeout from Taco Heaven, she decided to talk to him about it.

"Scarlet asked me if I would contribute to a project she's working on," Helena said.

"Really? That's interesting. Is it budgeting tips? You're really good at that," Malcolm said.

She smiled as he passed her a Dos Equis from the fridge.

"Thanks, babe, but that's not it. She wants me to help her curate a wedding planning subscription box to go out to her mailing list and talk about stress and how to deal with it," Helena said.

"Oh," he said, looking over at her. She knew that his gambling and how he'd dipped into their wedding fund to cover his losses were still shameful for him and hoped that she wasn't striking a nerve. "Well, I have to say you're good at that, too."

"I won't mention any specifics… Actually, I was going to suggest that we write the text for the insert together. We have to just talk about why we chose the products. Maybe talk about how pretending nothing is wrong leads to a bad situation or something like that," Helena said.

Malcolm was her partner in life and even though they weren't officially married yet, the two of them had a strong bond—even stronger since everything had come out about his gambling and they'd taken steps to deal with it together.

"I'd like that," he said, pulling her into his arms, lifting her up onto the kitchen island and stepping between her legs. "You're still much too good for me."

She laughed. "Don't worry, I won't let you forget it."

He kissed her and one thing led to another. Ultimately they had to reheat their tacos in the microwave before they ate them but neither minded.

Monthly poker night was a tradition in his group of friends. Until Scarlet had come along, it had been his only activity outside of polo that wasn't strictly work-related. He'd always looked forward to it. It was a traveling game, and everyone took turns hosting it. Malcolm was supposed to host tonight but since he had been dealing with overcoming his gambling addiction he'd dropped out of the game. It made him feel better and it definitely reassured Helena, according to Bianca, who had given Alec an earful when he'd mentioned his view that harmless betting with friends wasn't the same thing as gambling huge sums of money.

He hadn't realized how insensitive the comment was until she'd pointed it out. Betting of any kind was too much of a temptation for Malcolm. Alec felt like an awful friend for not recognizing that so he'd suggested pool tonight at the Five Families Clubhouse instead. That way Malcolm could join them. The rest of their group had agreed to pool instead of poker, so Alec was heading up there to spend the evening with the guys.

"Are you sure you don't mind me going?" Alec asked Scarlet as they were sitting on the couch in her house. Siobahn had taken over the large armchair catty-corner to the sofa and looked over at him shaking her head.

"She doesn't mind, dude. We're planning girls' night," Siobahn said.

"She's right, we are having girls' night and I'm fine," Scarlet said.

She had her legs draped over his lap and he rubbed her calf. She'd gone to the local pediatrician earlier and her visit—the first he'd accompanied her on—had revealed slightly elevated blood pressure. The doctor had advised her to stay off her feet so Alec had come to her house tonight.

It was hard to reconcile his feelings for her, which were more complicated than any he'd experienced before. And let's face it, he thought, he wasn't the most touchy-feely of men. He preferred to be in his dark office, with three computer monitors running different codes and algorithms to actually trying to decipher what his emotions meant. But he couldn't stop thinking about Scarlet. He'd cut back on some of his client meetings to stay closer to her as she transitioned from the first trimester into the second.

He hadn't told his parents about the baby yet because Scarlet wanted to wait. In fact, he'd mentioned it just to Mo because his twin was the only one he trusted to keep it quiet. Not that Bianca or his other brothers would intentionally spill the news. But he wasn't sure he was ready for anyone else to know about the baby. Right now it was their little secret. Just between him and Scarlet and the few people they trusted. If he told his parents, his dad was going to ask what their plans were. Were they going to get married or live together? His mom... She was always pressuring his brothers and him to settle down, so she'd push hard for him to make this permanent.

And he had no idea if that would work.

Her friends still weren't sure about him. And while Billie had gone back to New York, Siobahn was still here and had made it clear she still wasn't certain he was good enough for her friend. Given that Siobahn was still recovering from her breakup, that made a bit of sense. She was hiding out while she recovered from her broken heart. And he was doing everything possible to assure Scarlet and her friends that he was a decent guy.

But he also knew that he was afraid of how he could fit into her life. That if they were a couple he wasn't going to be able to avoid her high-profile lifestyle.

White lies had always seemed like something that weren't really harmful. He thought about the number of times he and Mo had pulled the switch before and they'd never thought about the consequences, but this time it had impacted both of their lives in ways neither of them had anticipated. He never wanted to put anyone through that again. He'd hurt Scarlet and Hadley, something he never would have thought he'd do.

He always prided himself on being a gentleman, so it had been difficult to see himself as the bad guy.

"Fair enough. Who's coming over?" he asked.

"Bianca, Helena, Hadley, Kinley and maybe Ferrin. She and Hunter are driving home tonight. It's the start of the term break." Lulu was curled up on Scarlet's lap but then jumped down and trotted across the room to her chair, where Scarlet kept a cashmere blanket for her.

"Sounds like fun. Are the kids coming?"

"No. Derek is babysitting," Scarlet said.

Alec chuckled at the thought. The onetime most eligible bachelor and notorious playboy had certainly changed a lot since he'd married Bianca. Alec liked the change for his sister's sake. She'd been burned badly once by love so it was nice to see her so happy now.

"Do you need me to do anything before I leave?" Alec asked.

"I think lending me your housekeeper to cook meals for us and to keep me company is enough," Scarlet said.

He shifted out from under her legs and leaned over to kiss her. As always when he touched her, he felt the tingling of desire burning through him. "If you need me, text me."

"I will," she promised, touching his jaw with her finger. "I'll be fine."

"Good."

"Bye, Siobahn," he said, as he straightened and walked out of the room.

She waved in his direction but didn't take her eyes off the notepad on her lap. Scarlet had explained that her friend was busy writing lyrics for a new album. Scarlet thought it was an improvement over partying every night so Siobahn could forget her ex.

"See you later," Scarlet said.

He nodded, not sure he could trust his voice. Because for the first time he had someone he wanted to come home to. It should have been nothing, really. This was a normal, everyday thing for people everywhere but for him it was different.

He drove to the clubhouse thinking about the future and realizing that he was starting to see himself with Scarlet. That the idea of having a family was no longer something foreign that made him feel like an impostor. And he wasn't sure what that meant.

Scarlet stood in the doorway of the family room watching Siobahn laugh with Helena and it made her smile. Of course she hadn't intended to get pregnant but it had led her to something that she never knew existed. It wasn't just this Texas town. It was a lifestyle she'd never realized she'd actually like. As good as it had been for her, she could see Cole's Hill working its magic on Siobahn, too. Her friend was recovering from her heartbreak in a healthy way and Scarlet had to wonder if it would have helped Tara to be in a place like this, too.

For once her sister's voice was quiet in the back of her mind and she wasn't sure if that was a good thing or not. One of the hardest parts about losing someone she loved was trying to hold on to that person. Trying not to let the memories fade. Her therapist had said she should just accept whatever felt right, but a part of her didn't want to ever let go of Tara.

"Hey, you okay?" Bianca said, coming up next to her.

"Yes. How about you? Your due date is getting close, isn't it?" Scarlet asked.

Bianca's stomach was large on her small frame and though she smiled easily, there were moments when Scarlet thought she noticed fatigue in her new friend. "Not soon enough."

"I'm not sure what I'm going to do when I get to that stage," Scarlet admitted.

"I don't want to alarm you but I haven't seen my feet in weeks and they are constantly swollen. Last night Derek had to help me get out of bed to go to the bathroom. I'm just so big now," Bianca said. "I don't remember being this big with Benito."

Scarlet felt panic rising in the back of her throat as Bianca talked about her late-stage pregnancy. She felt a little queasy and started to see spots dancing in front of her eyes. Damn. She was going to pass out if she wasn't careful.

"I have to sit down."

Bianca's eyes widened, and she put her arm around Scarlet, leading her to one of the armchairs. "I'm sorry. I shouldn't have said any of that."

Bianca used her foot to push a small footstool over toward Scarlet. "Prop your feet on here. I'm going to get you a damp towel for your neck. Put your head back and breath. I'm so sorry."

"You okay?" Hadley asked, coming over to Scarlet.

"Yes. Just not adjusting to the Texas heat as well as I'd hoped," Scarlet said, seizing on the weather as an excuse.

"I was going to get her a damp towel," Bianca said.

"I'll get it, Bia. You stay here."

Scarlet closed her eyes and put her head back. She

had been so busy thinking about what she should do once the baby was born she hadn't even considered the actual birth. Damn. She wasn't sure she could do it. Frankly, what Bianca had described wasn't something she wanted to experience...ever.

"I really shouldn't have said anything. I'm so miserable that I didn't even think... God, someone gag me. I just can't stop talking," Bianca said.

Scarlet had to laugh at that. She reached over to squeeze Bianca's hand. "It's okay. I mean I'd rather hear the truth than think it's going to be some dreamy perfect feeling."

"Me, too. The first time... Well, Jose wasn't around, and it was much harder on my own," Bianca said. She sat down in the chair next to Scarlet.

"I hope you don't mind but Alec did tell me the reason why," Scarlet said.

"I don't mind. I mean, at the time I was horrified. I had that big, televised wedding... I'm sure you know what that's like. Everyone saw it and I was really embarrassed by how fake it had become."

Scarlet definitely got that. "I try really hard to think of all my social media stuff as a job. When I film, I think of it as getting dressed up for the day. I'm still me but I'm playing a part. Then when I'm home I'm the real me... But if I had a wedding like yours, it would have been hard. I loved it, by the way. My sister and I watched the entire thing. It was a gorgeous wedding."

"Thank you," Bianca said. "I had hoped to transition into doing more lifestyle modeling after it, you know, a prettied up version of my real life, focusing on being a new mother and all of that, but with my marriage breaking down and the baby, it just never happened."

"I'm working with Kinley and Helena to do some subscription wedding boxes… Would you be interested in sponsoring a month? You would be perfect for a fairy-tale wedding planning one and then maybe you could keep it real by talking about living in the actual world after all that fantasy," Scarlet said.

Hadley came back and handed Scarlet a glass of water and the damp towel, which she placed on the back of her neck. "I love the wedding box idea. I hope it's ready before I get much further into planning mine. Do you have one for dealing with moms who want to take over the entire thing?"

Bianca and Scarlet both laughed at that. Hadley's mom was definitely having a moment with two engaged daughters and enjoying planning both of them.

"Not yet," Scarlet admitted. "We will have to do one."

She continued talking to the other women and started to feel sort of normal again, but in the back of her mind was the reminder that no matter how much she was enjoying her time in Cole's Hill, it was just a short interlude before she was going to have to return to her real life. Bianca's comments tonight had made her realize she needed to make a decision about Alec, so she could start figuring out the pregnancy and childbirth part.

She liked his family and his hometown. So, if they weren't going to be together, the thought of asking him to raise their child was becoming harder because each time she pictured that future she imagined herself with him. And she wasn't sure that she'd fit in. Right now when she was out of control and adrift it was easier to think of letting Alec raise their baby alone, but she had started to change and she only wished she could trust herself and believe that she could be a good mother. But had she ever been good enough at anything except scandal?

Twelve

The Five Families Club house was adjacent to an eighteen-hole golf course, tennis courts and the community swimming pool. Growing up, Alec had spent most summers at the clubhouse, charging things on his family's account and playing with his brothers and the friends he still had today. The area was named after the five families that had originally inhabited Cole's Hill. Wanting their town to be different from the others in the area, they'd established a close bond and had often driven their cattle up to Fort Worth Stockyards together back in the frontier days.

"You're looking…different tonight," Mauricio said, coming up to him and handing him a Lone Star beer.

His brother had always seemed like he had too much energy, like he was going to explode if he didn't keep moving. Their mom had often said that they were yin and yang to each other. But since Mo and Hadley had gotten engaged, his brother was calmer. Alec wanted to know what had made the difference but tonight wasn't the time to ask.

Alec took a long swallow and then glanced around to see if anyone was close enough to hear their conversation. The coast was clear; Mal and Diego were off in a corner discussing the upcoming polo match on Sunday and new strategies for the game. "It's Scarlet. Her blood pressure is a little high. I'm worried about her. I had been thinking of the—" he dropped his voice lower "—baby as something that we had time to adjust to and had completely forgotten that pregnancy can be complicated. And things between us are just starting to gel, you know?"

Mo clapped him on the shoulder and squeezed. "I get it. That's how I continue to feel with Hadley and she's even worse than I am. We both want this perfect version of life but it's not that way… It's messy and complicated. I don't want to sound like a sap but do you feel like you two are a team?"

"A team?"

"Yeah, like sometimes when things get really stressful I know I can turn to Hadley and just vent or other times I don't have to say it, she can see I'm on the verge of losing it and she helps me destress. I do the same thing for her."

"I don't know. It's hard to really tell. We are getting closer, but you know me… I'm not really good at reading people," Alec said.

"I am. And she watches you like she cares about you," Mo said.

"I think we like each other. How did you know things were different this time with Hadley? I mean, you broke up after high school and then got back together, and did it again after graduating college, and then again when she moved to New York."

Mo shook his head. "I didn't, bro. I was just winging it and trying like hell to control my temper. Then I started to realize instead of being angry…that part of me, well, Hadley calmed me down and was exactly what I was missing in my life."

"I don't have the anger you always did," Alec said.

"No you have a different kind of thing… Maybe emptiness?" Mo asked.

He shrugged. But his twin was right on the money. There had always been an emptiness inside him that he didn't know how to fill. But Scarlet was starting to fill it… Maybe that was what had him so off-kilter. Because she hadn't indicated that there was any reason for her to stick around after the baby.

"What are you two talking about?" Diego asked, coming over to them with Malcolm on his heels.

"Relationships."

"So it's getting serious with Scarlet?" Malcolm asked.

"Yes, but I know she's only in town temporarily. I mean, we've only been together for six weeks," Alec said, rubbing the back of his neck and taking another long swig of his beer. This discussion wasn't what he'd intended for the evening.

"Six weeks can be a lifetime in some relationships. Helena and I dated a long time before we got married but I knew on our second date that she was the one," Malcolm said. "Then I had to figure out how to up my game so that when I asked her she'd have no choice but to say yes."

"How did you up your game?" Diego asked. "Pippa and I started out with lust and then, well, things sort of happened."

"Things sort of happened?" Mo asked, jokingly. "You're such a romantic, bro."

"You know what I mean," Diego said. "Some women don't care as much about the words. It's action that matters."

"You have a point," Mo said, laughing.

Actually, his older brother did have a point. Was he worrying this entire situation to death? Trying to make something out of it that wasn't there? She was here and she was pregnant and they were together.

"I agree, but I want to add one thing, Alec. Helena didn't need me to up my game. She'd been ready since that second date, too. She'd just been afraid to tell me," Malcolm said. "Sometimes in love you have to take a risk."

"Wow, I'm a few minutes late and I walk in on a therapy session," Bart said as he approached.

"Hey, not all of us can rely on an accent to charm women," Alec said, going over to give Bart a one-armed hug.

"It's not just the accent, *mi amigo*," Bart said. "I can try to teach you boys, but I think it might be something you're born with."

There was a lot of good-natured ribbing as they started playing pool. Alec realized that despite the fact that he hadn't really told them the entire situation with Scarlet, his friends had given him some solid advice.

Now if he could figure out a way to charm Scarlet into staying in Cole's Hill. Into believing that he'd make a good father for their baby and that he was worth the risk of staying here.

He went to take another swallow of his beer and realized it was empty. The clubhouse kept the bar and the fridge behind it fully stocked in the pool rooms so he went and grabbed another drink. He had a lot to think about and the answer wasn't that hard to figure out. He needed to ask Scarlet to stay or at least to stay in his life.

Scarlet was surprised when she opened the door and saw Mrs. Velasquez standing there with Lulu at her heels two days later. The dog barked once and then when Mrs. Velasquez leaned down to pet her, stood up on her back legs and just watched her. Alec's mom was a morning news presenter in Houston and commuted to the city every day. So on her days off—according to Alec—she usually spent her time chilling out. But here she was on Scarlet's doorstep. Though the two women had met before, they really hadn't spent much time alone talking.

"Hello, Scarlet. I'm sorry for the intrusion. I was wondering if you could spare a few minutes to chat with me."

"I can," Scarlet said as her dog danced around her feet. "I was actually about to take this one for a walk. Would you like to join me?"

"That would be nice," Mrs. Velasquez said.

"Come on inside while I get her harness and leash, Mrs. Velasquez," Scarlet said, stepping back into the foyer.

"Please call me Elena."

"Of course," Scarlet said. "Is everything okay?"

"Yes… It's just I haven't had a chance to get to know you and I know you and Alec have been spending a lot of time together…"

"And?"

"And I wanted a chance to just chat with you. Bianca said you're funny and smart and I think I was a bit jealous," Elena said with a laugh.

Scarlet realized that Alec's mom was here to see

what kind of woman she was. How she would suit her son. And it was interesting—she didn't think she'd ever been in a situation like this before.

She got the dog's leash and they started out on their walk. The weather today was a bit cooler but not really cold.

They made small talk about the town and the upcoming open-air movie night in the park and then finally Elena stopped walking and sighed. "My husband said don't go over there, you'll make things awkward, and I hate to admit it but he was right, wasn't he?"

Scarlet shrugged. "I think so. I'm not sure what you want to know about me."

"I don't know, either. I miss out on what goes on in the daily routine of my kids and my husband because I do the morning news show and I'm gone a lot. And I didn't get a chance to know you at the polo match. It just wasn't the right time. I should have invited you to lunch or something," Elena said, tucking a strand of hair behind her ear.

"I pretty much grew up without my mother, so I have no idea how to deal with situations like this," Scarlet admitted. Talking about her mom always made her feel hollow and empty.

"I'm sorry to hear that," Elena said. "I did know your mom had passed away… I read your bio online, and am familiar with your TV show. Seems like you've had your share of tragedy."

Scarlet wasn't sure where this was leading and she didn't really want to talk to Alec's mom, but she wasn't going to be rude. Plus, she and Alec had had a paternity test just to resolve the issue and make sure there were no lingering questions, so she could speak with absolute assurance if the subject came up with Mrs. Velasquez.

"I have, but I'm sure that's not why you wanted to chat," Scarlet said. She wondered if Elena knew she was pregnant. Scarlet had the tiniest belly but it wasn't visible beneath the baggy top she had on.

"It isn't. Bianca shared your news with me and, of course, I know I should wait until Alec wants to tell me, but I've been a career woman who has been pregnant and I know that there are other considerations… Anyway, I just wanted to let you know I'm here if you need someone to talk to. I realize you don't have a mom and I know you are very capable but… Oh, Lord, I'm rambling."

Scarlet was upset that Bianca had told her mother. She turned to face the older woman and saw the concern and worry on her face. She'd felt attacked a moment earlier but now she realized that Elena was concerned.

"It wasn't Bianca's news to share," Scarlet said.

"I know. I tried to pretend I didn't know but frankly that's not the way I'm wired and after I realized you didn't have your mom…well, I thought you might need someone. And I know you don't know me but I want to fix that."

Scarlet also thought she saw a bit of joy. Elena might be the first person to see this baby just as a source of joy. Unlike Alec and her, who had been busy trying to figure out what to do next.

"It's okay. I was trying to keep it quiet as I'm not sure I'm ready for it to get out on social media."

"Bianca swore me to secrecy, but I just couldn't keep away," Elena said. "I want us to try to have a relationship. It's different with Bianca because I can just show up at her house and boss her around, but I won't do that with you."

Elena Velasquez was funny, Scarlet realized. And really sweet. "I'd like that. I'm not sure how long I'm going to stay in Cole's Hill. I sort of just came to give Alec the news… Well, I actually thought he was Mo at first."

"My boys really can be dumb sometimes," Elena said. "Would you like to have lunch? Maybe once a week. We can do it my house or wherever you like."

"Okay," Scarlet said. "That sounds nice. Thank you, Elena."

"No, thank you. I know I came over unannounced and then proceeded to be a meddlesome mom but I'm not someone who can just sit by and wait… But I won't be too pushy. Well, I am pushy, but you can always tell me to back off," Elena said.

Scarlet nodded. Her mom hadn't been around

since she was a child and she had very few relationships with women who weren't her age or just a few
years older, so this was different. They started walking again and Elena was more relaxed talking about
current events and life around Cole's Hill. She admitted to being glad she worked in Houston, so she
could sometimes escape from the bustle of small-
town gossip.

After Elena left, Scarlet tried not to let the feeling of melancholy bother her. If her father had been
a different sort of man, if he'd married a woman like
Elena… But he hadn't. It was nice to have Elena now,
but she didn't need a mom. Her child would have a
grandmother who wanted to be in the baby's life,
and that was something she'd never thought was a
priority before.

But did Scarlet have what it took to be the baby's
mother?

Alec had asked his housekeeper to make sure the
garden and pool area looked like something out of
a romantic fantasy tonight. She'd sent him several
pictures from which to choose and she'd hit it out of
the park. The entire backyard had been lit with fairy
lights in the trees and bushes. There was music playing through the landscape speakers and a thick carpet
had been laid in the sitting area under the portico.

He took one more look at everything before he
left to go and pick Scarlet up. Mal had been right the

other night when he'd said that waiting sometimes wasn't the answer. Alec had been letting his fear dictate his silence with Scarlet. He wanted them to be a couple, and while he was the first to admit that there was no way they were going to have everything sorted out before the baby came, they were certainly on the path to that.

So he'd done it. Pulled the trigger and gone to the jewelers in Houston to buy her a ring. He'd planned a night that would show her how much she'd come to mean to him. He could work from anywhere in the world. Unlike his brother Diego, who had to stay in Cole's Hill because of the ranch and his horses, Alec's job was pretty much online. So he could be wherever Scarlet needed to be.

He knew his parents might not like that; his mom especially preferred that they all lived in Cole's Hill. But she also was realistic. He'd stopped by his parents' house the night before to talk to them about it. Though it would be embarrassing if she said no, he couldn't ask a woman to share his life without telling his parents about her, the baby and how he wanted a life that he might have with Scarlet.

He ran his hands down the side of his dress pants, felt the ring in his pocket and realized his hands were shaking.

He had also given Mo a heads-up about his plans, but his twin said he'd already seen it coming. Alec wasn't sure if that was true or not.

He took his time driving to Scarlet's house to pick her up. He parked in front and fiddled with the in-car audio system so that when they got back in the vehicle, the song that had been playing the first time they danced would come on. It wasn't a particularly romantic song—"Hey Ma" by Pitbull and J Balvin—but it was their first song.

He flipped down the mirror to check that his hair was in place and then got out of the car. He'd never felt so nervous. Then Scarlet opened the door and he saw her standing there in a cocktail dress with her hair up. Simply put, she was the most beautiful woman he'd ever seen.

She was everything that he hadn't realized he'd been looking for and suddenly he understood what Mal had meant when he said he needed to up his game. When he stood there staring at Scarlet, he had to wonder if he was good enough for her. Most of the time he was a good man but there were days when he did what he had to in order to get by. He could improve…not that she'd asked him to.

"I've never known you to be so quiet," she said in greeting.

"You're gorgeous tonight. I just can't believe that you're mine," he said at last.

"Am I yours?" she asked with an arched eyebrow.

"I hope so. I like thinking of us as a couple," he admitted. And frankly, if she didn't, then this entire night was going to go downhill fast.

"I like it, too," she said. "You're looking very dashing tonight. Who knew you owned a tux."

"I was wearing one the night we met," he reminded her, putting his hand on the small of her back as they walked down the steps that led to the driveway and his car.

"It was your brother's," she reminded him.

"You're never going to let me live that down, are you?"

"Never," she said with a smile.

He opened the door for her and couldn't help but let his gaze linger on her legs as she swung them into the car. He went around to the driver's side, got behind the wheel and started the engine. "Hey Ma" started playing and she looked over at him.

"Wasn't this the song that was playing at the gala?"

"It was. I know it's cheesy, but I think of it as our song," he said.

She smiled over at him. "You're a closet romantic, Alec."

"I have my moments," he admitted.

"You sure do," she said, as he put the car in gear.

She put her hand on his thigh as he drove through the neighborhood and he started to relax. The nerves that had been dogging him since he'd shown up at her front door were starting to dissipate.

When they got to his house, he escorted her to the front door and then swung it open and stepped back for her to enter. He'd lined the floor with rose petals, something Hadley had promised him looked romantic, and had his housekeeper light candles in Scarlet's signature scent, which he'd tracked down via her assistant, Billie, who'd been surprisingly helpful.

"Alec… This is so romantic."

"Well, I wanted this night to be special," he said. "We've been seeing each other for a while now and I wanted to show you how much you've come to mean to me."

He closed the door behind himself and she turned toward him, putting her hand on his chest and going up on her tiptoes. Their eyes met.

"You mean a lot to me, too."

Thirteen

Scarlet had never had a man try to romance her like this, and it touched her. She felt that warm sensation in her stomach that made her wonder if she loved him. Love was the one thing she'd always tried to avoid. She'd loved Tara, of course, but that was it. Tara been the one person she'd been unable to keep herself from caring too much about.

Alec was different. There was no reason to love him. They weren't related, and they didn't have any bonds between them other than the child and the ones that they'd created over the last six weeks as they'd gotten to know each other.

She slowly followed the path of roses toward the

back of his house and caught her breath when she looked out at his patio and garden. It had been transformed.

He made you an Eden, Tara's voice whispered through her mind.

The Princess Diaries had been their favorite movie to watch and she knew immediately what her sister meant. He'd made this ordinary suburban backyard seem otherworldly. And she knew in her heart of hearts that she cared deeply for him. More deeply than she'd ever cared for anyone before.

She almost wished she didn't. That she could enjoy the fantasy of this and go back to pretending that she was addicted to him because addiction was dangerous and unhealthy. Looking at it that way, it would make sense to want to escape this. But romance… Well, it would make her look silly if she turned and ran away.

If she let the panic rising up inside her have free rein.

"I had my chef prepare dinner for us," he said, holding out a chair at the table for her.

Dinner. It was just dinner, she thought as she sat down. She could handle this.

He sat next to her and poured her some sparkling water over ice, adding some fresh strawberries the way she liked it. He was the kind of person who noticed details. She liked that about him.

"Your mom stopped by to see me," she said when

they were eating. She'd been unsure of how to bring it up to Alec. He hadn't mentioned a future together and she'd been trying to keep the baby and them separate. And once she'd met his mom, it had been even harder to think of not being a part of her baby's life. "I meant to text you earlier but she knows about the baby."

"Oh, well, I was going to tell my parents soon but wanted to figure out what we were doing first," he said. "I know they're going to have a lot of questions that you and I haven't really been ready to answer."

She nodded. "Yeah. She said she knew I didn't have a mom and wanted to get to know me."

"You can tell her no," Alec said. "She's a bit—"

"Pushy," Scarlet said. "She told me. But honestly she was so sweet I liked it."

"Good. My parents, as you've seen, are the type to get involved in everything."

"Yeah, it's kind of funny but I noticed they sort of parent all of your friends, too," Scarlet said. Her father was more the hit-on-her-friends type, which was kind of what she thought the norm was until she'd come to Cole's Hill. Of course, she'd seen families like the Velasquezes on TV and in the movies but they'd never seemed real to her.

"They do. Mainly I think it's because we all grew up around here and they've known all of my friends since they were little kids," Alec said.

"I like it," she said. "I think Tara would have liked it, too."

"I wish I'd met her," Alec said. "She was very important to you, wasn't she?"

"Yes."

"What was the craziest thing you two did growing up?" he asked. "Mo and I were always in trouble so our kid is going to get the mischief gene."

Our kid.

Like they were a couple.

Panic started to rise in her, laced with a bit of hope that she didn't even acknowledge.

Tell him about me, Tara's voice whispered.

"She was always good at surprising me with something fun. We went to different boarding schools and the year after our mom died, I was pretty miserable. One night I was lying in my bed at the dorm when I heard this scratching at the window.

"I opened it up and glanced down to see Tara standing down below. She had this large branch in her hands and had been scraping it across the glass."

Scarlet took a sip of her drink.

"She waved at me to come out and I sneaked down to meet her. She took my hand and we ran as fast as we could to a taxi she had waiting and she ordered him to take us to the beach. It was the middle of the winter, freezing cold, because my school was in Massachusetts. But when we got to the beach, we went and stood on the sand and waited. And I asked her what we were waiting for and she said we'd see Mom's angel at sunrise."

"That sounds wonderful," Alec said. "I wish my brother were so thoughtful. Instead, Mo smacked me on the head with a pillow until I woke up one time so I could hand him his stuffed dog, Scratchers, who'd fallen out of the top bunk."

"Poor baby. Mo is such a bully," Scarlet said, jokingly.

"Yeah, he was. But Tara sounds like she took care of you," Alec said.

"Sometimes. She had her own problems, too. One time she deliberately crashed her sunfish sailboat into mine to keep me from winning a Fourth of July regatta at our yacht club."

"That I can relate to. Inigo was always superfast on bikes or go-carts or even golf carts so we'd sometimes crash into him to keep him from winning… But it hasn't hurt him. It probably made him even better at racing," Alec said.

"I'm sure."

"Have you ever thought about having more kids?" he asked. "Or do you think this one will be it?"

He had a right to ask her that question, she thought, but at the same time she didn't want to answer. She wasn't even sure what she was going to do about the baby she carried right now. "I haven't. I'm not at all ready to think about that."

"Fair enough. I'm not, either. I just didn't know if

you dreamed of a big family," he said, clearing away the dinner dishes.

"I didn't dream of a family at all. I figured I'd be doing my thing by myself forever," she said.

"Ready for dessert?" he asked because he wasn't sure how to react to her answer.

"I'm good for now," she said.

"Okay."

He sat back down and they both sort of stared at each other. She wished she could read his mind. Know what he was thinking. This dinner he'd asked her to dress up for was more than just their usual get-together. And he was coming to mean more to her than she wanted to really admit.

"You really outdid yourself tonight," she said.

"I know it's over the top but you're the first woman I've ever wanted to do this stuff for," he said. "You mean a lot to me, Scarlet."

She nodded. What was she going to say? She had to think and fast because she was starting to want to stay. Here in Cole's Hill. Here with Alejandro Velasquez. Here with this family she'd always secretly craved.

He might not know it but he was offering her everything she'd always believed she'd never find. And it was harder than she thought to keep her cool. She swallowed hard, feeling the tears burning in her eyes as he opened the French doors to the patio and she heard the sound of jazz music playing. She'd told him she loved jazz and he'd remembered.

He's good for you, Tara's voice whispered again. *Don't mess this up.*

Don't mess it up.

That was exactly what she was so afraid of doing.

"Thank you," she said as she stepped onto the patio. She saw that he had new carpet in the seating area, a thick Berber rug that looked really soft. She toed off her shoes and stepped onto it.

The smell of roses and jasmine mingled in the air. She turned to check on Alec and noticed he was watching her. She held her hand out to him as "'S Wonderful" started playing and he came to join her, drawing her into his arms, singing under his breath as he danced them around in a circle. His hands against her back were warm and strong, his touch turning her on the way it always did.

His slightest touch was all it took to inflame her senses and make her forget everything but his dark chocolate eyes and his rock-hard body. He dipped her as the song ended and she clung to him, confident he wouldn't drop her because Alec was strong. He was always there for her. And as much as she didn't want to depend on him, she realized she already did. Whether she wanted to admit it to herself or not, she already felt deep affection for him.

Affection? Tara's voice jeered. *Why can't you admit you love him?*

She pulled herself from Alec's embrace and turned away from him—and from the voice in her head. No way was she going to admit it, but the truth was there echoing in each beat of her racing heart.

She wasn't lovable.

She never had been.

Her mom had left her.

Her sister had disappeared first into addiction and then died.

Her father couldn't even be bothered to speak to her unless he needed her signature on a document.

How was she going to believe that she could love Alec and be loved in return?

"Scarlet, baby? Are you okay?" he asked.

The concern in his voice made her feel dumb. She wasn't reacting the right way. She never knew how to behave in this situation. Give her a bunch of paparazzi standing outside her front door trying to catch her in an embarrassing situation and she could handle it. But a guy who'd planned a romantic evening—no dice.

"I'm not," she said, shaking her head. "I just realized that I've been pretending all this time that you and I could be a real couple."

"What? What do you mean? I wanted to make this night special… I'm not like this normally."

She shook her head. "I know. That makes it even worse. I want to be the kind of woman you deserve, Alec. Someone who can see all this and feel safe enjoying it, but I'm not. Nothing in my life prepared me for this. I'm chaos and ruin. I'm running from one hot mess to the next and I don't think I can change."

He shook his head, holding his hands out toward her. "You don't have to change. I'm not asking you to."

But he was. He might not have said the words, but he wanted something permanent between them, and that scared her more than anything else. She had to get out of here, out of Texas before she forgot the truth of who she was. That she was Scarlet O'Malley of the hard-drinking, always fighting O'Malleys. Not the woman who could settle into domestic life.

That wasn't her scene.

He had no idea how things had gotten so far out of his control. "Let's go inside."

She didn't budge, just stood there with her arms wrapped around her body, and he realized she was scared. He went over to her and hugged her, careful to be aware if she was resistant to his embrace. But she sighed and rested her forehead against his shoulder. Her breathing was ragged and rough as she stood there.

He rubbed his hand up and down her back.

"I have no idea what I've done to upset you. But I'm sorry. I'll try not to do it again," he said, remembering that first afternoon when they had been on the patio and she'd run away from him.

"I'm not that guy who lied to you the first night

we met. I've been trying to show you that I can be so much more than you first thought I was. But I know I still have a long way—"

"Stop. Alec, you're so much more than I ever expected you to be. Even when I thought you were Mo, Humanitarian of the Year, I couldn't have guessed at how perfect you really are."

He shook his head. "That's definitely not true. You don't have to spare my feelings, Scarlet. I know I'm not anyone's idea of a hero."

She lifted her head and their eyes met. "Stop. This is more about me than it is about you. I'm not this kind of woman. One who settles down."

She gestured to the table and the carpet, then to the speakers and the house. "But this makes me want to believe I am. All my life I've been pretty damn sure of who I am. I know I'm not everyone's cup of tea, but that's fine. I'm an O'Malley and I get by. This is different. This is changing my life to something that I've never had. I only ever had one-night stands before you. And it didn't bother me. I liked being unencumbered."

He nodded. He understood where she was coming from. "Everything changed the moment you got pregnant. We have to change to."

She nodded. "I don't know if I can. I don't know if I can be a mom. If I can be…whatever this is you want me to be. I was just starting to get used to sleeping with you and being here in your town, but this… It's too permanent. Things don't last, Alec. They never do."

Her words made him ache for her and angry at her at the same time. "I'm not your dad."

"I'm not saying you are," she snapped back at him.

She was full-on defensive, the way she'd been when he'd first seen her at the polo match. He had no idea what to say to diffuse the situation. How had he read it so wrong? He wasn't good with people, but this was a big misstep even for him.

"Don't be like that," he said. "I'm not attacking you."

"I know," she said, turning away from him. "This is how I get when I'm scared."

"What's scary about this?"

"Everything. Every. Damn. Thing."

He waited, hoping she'd continue, but she didn't.

"I can get rid of it all," he said, gesturing toward the candles, the rose petals, all the romantic trappings of the evening. "Will that help?"

"No, but mainly because I want it. I want to believe all of this and you. I want to have this feeling inside when I look at you and think about you and not be afraid that it's going to disappear."

"Then do. I'm not going anywhere…unless you want me to come to New York with you."

She gave him the saddest smile he'd ever seen and just shook her head. "I don't think you'd like it. My life isn't at all what we've had here in Cole's

Hill. And I've stayed too long. I forgot what I was here to do."

"What was that?"

"Find out if you were a decent guy who could raise my child without screwing it up or if I would need to find another family to do that," she said.

"What?"

"Don't be like that. It was a one-night stand, we didn't know each other at all," she said. "My family is completely f'd up and I don't want any child of mine to grow up the way I did. I wasn't sure what to do. I didn't know what I was going to encounter when I got here."

He took her hand in his, rubbing his thumb over her knuckles. He understood her fears, but surely they'd gotten past that. "But we do now."

"Yes, we do. And like I said earlier, you're more than I expected. And your family is a great support network. This baby will have everything I never did."

"So then why does the romance bother you? Do you want us to be more businesslike in how we are with each other but still sleep together?" he asked, because he thought he'd been moving them toward what she was describing.

She shook her head and walked back over to her shoes and put them on. "I am not going to be part of the child's life after I give birth."

"I'm not following," he said. "You want me to raise the child alone?"

"Yes. You're a much better person than I am. You know how to be a part of a family. You know how to raise a child. I'm—"

"Hell, no, I'm not," he said. He couldn't do that. Not on his own. He had thought they could do it together because they each brought something to the partnership that was different. But his raising the kid alone? What was she talking about? "I work late nights all the time. I can't be a single dad."

She nodded.

"Fair enough. I just want this child to have everything I can't give it. And, Alec, you are a very caring man. You'd be a great dad."

"You'd be a great mom, and I don't want to do it on my own. Won't you please consider doing this with me?" he asked. "Together I think we make a great team."

She didn't say anything and he realized that he had read her wrong. That whatever it was she'd been doing with him the last six weeks, it hadn't been establishing a relationship so that they could raise a family together. He was the person she saw as taking care of the child while she went back to New York, back to her social-media-driven life and away from him.

He didn't blame her for thinking that at first but they'd gotten to know each other. She had to realize that he wasn't going to be okay with that. Or maybe she didn't?

"I want us to try living together," he said. "I know you weren't thinking in those terms so I'm not in any hurry for your answer."

"I can't."

He was starting to get angry. "Make me understand this. I know you're not the kind of woman who would just walk away."

"I can't trust myself," she said at last. "What if I'm like my dad?"

"What if you're not?" he asked.

"I won't take a chance with our baby," she said.

Fourteen

"What do you mean? Alec, I'm not going to be this woman," she said, gesturing around the patio. "Our lives are very different. I came here because I needed to know if the father of my baby was a decent guy—"

"You keep saying that. But we've moved beyond that. You've become an important part of my life and I think you feel the same about me. We aren't two strangers figuring out a problem. We are two people who care deeply about each other."

Care deeply... The words echoed in her head and for once Tara's sarcastic voice was silent. And the panic that she'd mostly managed to forestall since the moment she'd found out she was pregnant started to rise inside her. A tsunami of doubt was swelling and making her aware of how ill prepared she was to have this conversation with Alec.

"I can't. I can't do this. I'm sorry. I'll be in touch in a few days. I need you to think about whether you want to raise this child without me or if we should look for another option," she said.

She walked around him and toward the house. Again, the smell of roses and jasmine surrounded her but this time it made her sad. This patio had been the place that had cemented their relationship and it was probably fitting that it was here that she was ending it. She had never been good at relationships and she wasn't truly sure why she'd stayed here so long.

The novelty of it?

Don't be daft, Tara's voice whispered through her mind. *You liked it and you love him.*

Love.

No way. She didn't love him. She wouldn't allow herself to. Everyone she'd ever loved had died.

"Scarlet!"

She glanced over her shoulder and she saw the agony and pain and anger in his eyes. In the way he stood there with his hands clenched in fists just watching her. There was a knot in her stomach and she just wanted to get far enough away from him that she could stop feeling this. She hated this.

"Don't go. Not like this," he said.

"I have to. You want something from me that I

can't give you and I should never have allowed myself to let this happen."

"You didn't allow it," he said. "There's a bond between us whether you want to admit it or not, and no matter where you go and what decisions you think you're making that bond will still be there."

She shook her head. That couldn't be true. She'd never been in that position before and she highly doubted that once she got back to New York and her old life that she wouldn't be able to move on from him.

She'd been playing a game while she was here. Pretending all along that she was someone like Mia in *The Princess Diaries* but knowing it was a fantasy she'd never be able to have in real life. This Eden wasn't for her. Not really. It was for some woman Alec thought she was.

"Thank you, Alec," she said at last. "Our time together was unexpected, and I enjoyed this while it lasted."

"Yeah, whatever," he said. "I'll drive you home."

"You don't have to," she said. She didn't know what she'd do if they were in the car together. She needed to get away. To be alone.

"Sorry, but you're pregnant with my baby and I'm not going to let you walk back to your house alone," he said. "I can call someone to pick you up if you'd prefer."

She debated it. If she stayed any longer, it was

only going to make this worse on both of them. The car ride would be over in minutes. She nodded.

"I'd appreciate the ride," she said.

"No problem. I was raised to be a gentleman," he said through clenched teeth as he walked past her and held open the French doors that led to his living room. She walked into his house and straight to the front door. She heard his footsteps behind her and then the rattle of his keys as he took them from the bowl on the foyer table. He reached around her to open the door and his arm brushed her shoulder.

She felt that delicious shiver of desire go through her and she turned to step away at the same time as he did. They bumped into each other, and when their eyes met, her heart broke. She knew that she was making the right choice for the baby but also for Alec. Everyone in her family had a major self-destruct mode when it came to love, and she knew she wasn't any different. She hated to see the pain on his face, hated to feel this heaviness in her own heart, but there was no other way.

This was bigger than herself. This was the only thing she could do to make sure her child didn't grow up like her. And that was the important thing. The pain would pass and fade despite what Alec had said.

"I hope…" She trailed off. What could she say? There weren't words to express what she wanted to say because the truth was, she hoped he could find happiness without her and she was pretty sure he would.

"Yeah, whatever," he said.

She realized that was his way of hiding his hurt. She also noticed as they walked to his car in the driveway that he'd never lashed out at her. He'd been angry but the meanest thing he'd ever said was that their bond was strong, and she might not get over it. Which was hardly mean. He was a great guy. The kind of man she wanted for her own but was too afraid to claim.

That just made her love him more.

Damn. She did love him.

Which made it all the more important that she get away from him. For both of their sakes. Whenever she wanted something she turned destructive. He drove her home in silence and when he pulled up to her house, she opened her car door herself, putting her hand on his arm to stop him from coming around to help her out.

"Goodbye, then," she said.

"Yeah, goodbye," he replied. She closed the car door as she got out and then stepped away as he gunned the engine and disappeared into the night.

Alec knew he wasn't in the best shape to be attending a family dinner. It had been six weeks since Scarlet had left Cole's Hill. She'd instructed her attorney to contact his attorney, Ethan Caruthers, to keep him informed of the baby's progress. She had also conveyed via letter that she hoped he'd reconsider and raise the baby on his own, or she'd have to consider other options like adoption. Ethan had counseled him to think of the child but Alec was convinced. He wasn't the kind of man who could raise a child on his own. Other options worried him and he didn't want to give up his child any more than he thought that Scarlet did.

But his mom wasn't happy with that decision and so he wasn't surprised that his dad was waiting for him on the front porch in one of the rockers when he arrived at his childhood home. His father had a bottle of tequila sitting on the table between the two chairs on a bar tray that also had salt, wedges of lime and shot glasses.

"Dad," Alec said by way of greeting.

"Son, take a seat."

"I really don't want to," he said. In fact, he should leave. He wasn't ready to talk to his family or anyone else. He wished he could say he was mad because that at least would make sense. But instead he was hurt and he still woke up every night reaching for Scarlet even knowing she'd never be next to him in his bed again.

"Tough shit," his father said. "Take a seat, Alejandro."

"Dad—"

"I'm not asking," he replied.

Alec sat down in the empty chair and refused to look at his father. Over the course of his life, he'd had exactly five conversations with his father on this porch. Three of them had occurred when he was under the age of eighteen. One of them took place after he'd screwed up royally in college, and then there was this one today. He knew his father saved the porch talks for stuff that he didn't want to bring into the house. The messy stuff that needed to be said.

"I'm not ready to talk about this," Alec said.

"That's fine. You just need to listen. But first, pour us both a shot," his father said.

Alec opened the bottle of tequila and poured two shots. His father licked his hand at the same time that Alec did. They took turns with the saltshaker, then picked up a wedge of lime each and then their shots. Alec licked the salt off his hand, downed his shot and then chased it with the lime. He put his glass down and then sat back in the Kennedy rocker.

"I don't know what's going on with you and Scarlet," his father said. "But your mom told me she's pregnant and you told me you were going to ask her to marry you. And she's gone so I'm guessing something happened."

"Yeah, she doesn't want this. She said she's not cut out for this kind of life and she wants me to raise the child on my own. That's why she came here."

"To check you out?" his father asked.

"Yes," he said, turning to face his father. He felt overcome with emotions and blinked because he really didn't want to lose it. Not now. "And we passed her test. She thinks our extended family would be great to raise the child. Yay for us. But I didn't pass her test."

His dad reached across the table and put his hand on Alec's shoulder. "What makes you think you didn't?"

"She left. She made it clear that she's not into me," he said. "I sound like a complete dumbass, right? I should be able to say I've moved on. It's been six weeks, Dad, and I'm still not over her."

"Love's not like that. You don't get over it," he said. "Especially if it's real. Look at your brother and Hadley."

"I can't. Dad, I'm turning into a really nasty person on the inside. I hate that everyone else seems to be able to find happiness and I can't."

His father nodded. "You will find it."

"Not with her," he said at last.

"Not with her. Your mom told me a little bit about her family and it seems like she has her own issues to sort out," his dad said. "And you'll figure out how to move on. But your mom and I think you should raise the baby. We will help you. Your brothers will help you. And that child will probably help you, too."

Alec leaned forward, putting his elbows on his knees and then his face in his hands. Raise the baby?

That's what Scarlet wanted and he honestly had been so consumed by her rejection he hadn't spent much time allowing himself to think about the baby. But now that his father said it like that, he hated the thought of a Velasquez being raised by anyone else. He wasn't sure what he was doing but he'd figure it out.

"Okay," he said at last. "I'm not going to pretend I know what I'm doing but I'll let Ethan know I want custody."

"Good. Now about the girl," his father said, pouring two more shots of tequila. "What can we do there?"

"I don't know, Dad," Alec said. "She said she's not good at relationships. Hell, I'm not a poster boy for them, either."

"No, you're not. Maybe you need to show her what it would mean, being in a relationship with you."

His father had a cagey look on his face and Alec wasn't sure what his father had in mind.

"How?"

"Your mom's going to kill me for suggesting this, but why don't you move to New York and make sure she knows you're there."

"I don't know. I don't want to seem like a desperate loser," Alec said.

"Don't, then. Be there for the pregnancy and the baby. That's it. Once she sees you, she'll change her mind."

"I'm not so sure. I love her but is that enough to convince her?"

His dad smacked him on the back of the head. "Dammit, Alejandro. Love is the most powerful thing in the world. You just keep loving her until she realizes she loves you back."

"You think that will work?" he asked his father. Though he had seen firsthand how Diego and Mauricio had both won the women they loved.

"How do you think I won your mom over? She wanted a city slicker, not a horse rancher. Not even one who played polo. But I wore her down. Just kept asking her to marry me until she said yes."

Alec shook his head. It wasn't a bad plan, he thought. If he'd learned anything in the last six weeks, it was that his feelings for Scarlet had grown, not disappeared.

So that was it, then. He had a plan and some hope for the future. His dad had been right about being closer to Scarlet, but not in New York. That was her turf. He'd agree to raise the child but only if she came back here until she delivered. That would give him the home-field advantage, and hopefully the remaining time in her pregnancy would be enough to convince her that they were stronger together. He didn't allow himself to lose hope. He loved her too much for that.

Scarlet wasn't feeling it today but her film crew was due to arrive any minute. Since the shows were all filmed six months before they aired, she'd asked the crew and the film company to keep her pregnancy under wraps. And they agreed. She needed to figure out the situation with her child, and she needed to keep her pregnancy private to do that. Alec still wanted them both to be involved in the baby's life, and the longer she was carrying her child the harder it was to think of letting anyone raise the baby but Alec. In the middle of the night she sometimes pictured herself and Alec with the baby, but then the dreams twisted into that lifeless image of Tara when she'd died.

Her partners in the subscription box business loved the idea of a wedding/bride theme, but since she was pregnant they were pushing for her to do an expectant-mother-themed one, as well. The only problem was she didn't want to concentrate on that. The almost seven weeks since she'd left Cole's Hill hadn't been easy. Each day she missed Alec—and how was that even possible?

She'd left friends and homes and family a million times in her life and just moved on without looking back. Now all of a sudden she couldn't stop thinking about him. She had decided to communicate only through lawyers and by letter because she was afraid if she heard his voice she'd change her mind and run back to him.

And if it was just the two of them, she might risk it, but there was the baby to consider.

She put her hand on her stomach, which was definitely getting larger. She'd taken to wearing clothes in her apartment that showed off her baby bump. She liked the thought of the child, which was its own kind of torture. Billie had recommended that she reconsider giving the child to Alec. And the truth was she was reconsidering a lot. Life wasn't any easier now that she was back in New York.

"The film crew is here. Do you want to go down and get them?" Billie asked. "I think they want to do some outside shots."

"Will you go for me and tell them I can't do it today?"

"Sure, but you should probably leave the apartment. You're going to have to at some point."

"I know, but not yet," she admitted. She'd been hiding away, trying to make sense of her feelings. She didn't know what love should feel like but the way she longed for Alec, the way she missed him, made her believe this had to be something pretty close to it.

Scarlet bent down to scoop up Lulu, who was dancing around her feet. The little dog buried her face in the curve of Scarlet's neck as Scarlet petted her.

"How about if we go for a walk in Central Park when I get back?" Billie asked. "The weather isn't too bad today. It's supposed to snow, which you love, and you can put a coat on so the baby bump won't show if any paps snap a photo of you."

She looked at her friend and assistant and saw the concern on Billie's face. She'd also heard from Bianca, who had her baby—a little girl she'd named Aurora. Kinley, Hadley and Helena had all emailed and texted as well, just saying they missed her.

She missed them, as well.

You don't have to miss anyone, Tara's voice whispered through her mind. *Go back to Texas.*

Go back to Texas.

Was it that simple?

She stood there staring at Billie for a long minute and then nodded. She wasn't happy here. She knew she was due to start shooting, but for once in her life she wasn't going to share this with the world. Not until she won Alec back… If he'd still have her. She was in love with him and being apart wasn't really making her feel any better. She had absolutely no idea how to raise a child but with Alec by her side she'd feel a lot better about trying.

"Uh, that's a no on the park, Billie. How about if we go to Cole's Hill instead?" Scarlet said.

"About damned time," Billie said. "You have been miserable since you came home, and I think it's because you love Alec."

"I think I do, too," Scarlet said. "Go and deal with whoever is downstairs while I call the film company to reschedule shooting and call the pilot—"

"How are you going to deal with any of that? I'm the one with the numbers," Billie countered.

"Text them to me. Billie, I think I'm going to be a mom."

"You are going to be a mom," Billie said, coming over and hugging her. "And you're going to be great. Be right back."

Billie left the apartment and Scarlet picked up her phone and looked at the text messages. She hadn't heard from Alec since she'd left him that night. What was she going to say?

Tell him how you feel, Tara's voice whispered. *That's the one thing we never did in our family.*

Her sister was right. It was time to do the opposite of everything that she'd learned to do in order to protect herself from being hurt. It was time to be honest about her emotions and admit she needed Alec in her life. That she wanted the family that fate had dropped in her lap.

Fifteen

Ethan's law offices were in one of the new towers that had just been completed on the outskirts of town near Hadley's loft. Normally he took care of all of his business with Ethan at the Five Families Clubhouse or the Bull Pen. But Ethan had insisted that to get everything he wanted in the new deal with Scarlet, he was going to have to come into the office.

So he'd postponed a trip to Michigan to see one of his new clients and was now on his way to the lawyer's office. It had been three days since his conversation with his dad and Alec had been working nonstop to get everything in order so that when Scarlet came back to Cole's Hill he'd be able to focus on her. That was why rescheduling the client trip wasn't ideal. What if she was able to come back sooner than he thought? He definitely wanted to be here when she arrived.

But when he got to Ethan's office, Hadley was waiting in the parking lot and she looked upset.

He couldn't ignore his future sister-in-law, and Ethan would understand if Alec was late.

"You okay?"

"No, I'm not. Thank goodness you're here. I think there's a mouse in my loft," Hadley said. "I've texted Mo, but he said you were on your way to Ethan's. Could you go and check it out?"

"Sure," he said. "I thought you weren't living there anymore."

"I'm not but I've been working to get it ready so I can rent it out, and I have someone coming to look at it in like thirty minutes," Hadley said. "I swear, I can handle anything but a mouse. They are small and fast and I'm getting the heebie-jeebies just thinking about it."

"I got this. I'll go check it out and then figure out how to catch it," Alec said.

"Thank you," she said. "Should I tell Mo to still come?"

"Yes. He's going to have to figure out how to humanely dispose of it. Also, if there's one in the loft you should check your studio."

"I didn't even think of that," Hadley said. "Here are my keys. The front door code is 0322."

He nodded, taking her keys and walking toward the entrance to the lofts, which was around the side of the building where Hadley had her art studio. There was also a coffee house and a martial arts dojo. Ethan's offices were in the new high-rise adjacent to the lofts.

He keyed in the code and as soon as he stepped inside he saw the rose petals on the floor. They stirred memories of the night he'd been planning to ask Scarlet to marry him. He still couldn't believe it had gone so wrong. He followed the trail to the elevator. Obviously one of Hadley's neighbors had the same idea that Alec had and he hoped it worked out better for them than it had for him.

He took the elevator up to the residential area and when he got off he noticed the trail of rose petals continued down the hall ending at the door to Hadley's loft. He was starting to worry that his brother might be waiting for Hadley, and if there was one thing he didn't want to see it was his brother trying to be sexy for his fiancée.

He knocked on the door. "Mo? You in there? Uh, Hadley is downstairs. She thinks there's a mouse up here."

The door opened slowly and he saw that the petals made a path through the entire loft to form a giant heart in the middle of the floor. He stepped inside and turned as the door closed behind him.

His heart raced as he saw Scarlet standing there watching him. She wore a flowy dress that fell to her knees and had a V in the front. She looked so good it was hard to not go right to her and pull her into his arms. He noticed the tiny changes that pregnancy had made to her body and he smiled at her as she stood there.

"So… Turns out I'm not Mo," she said.

"I'm so glad. I wasn't looking forward to seeing my brother trying to be romantic with Hadley," he answered. He had a feeling that this was a good thing. Her being here in Cole's Hill before Ethan had even sent back his counteroffer seemed like really good news to him.

"Me, too. That would have been awkward," she said, twisting her fingers together, and he realized she was nervous. "But I wasn't sure you'd come if you knew it was me. Seems that I'm the kind of girl who likes this stuff."

She gestured to the rose petals and the heart she'd made in the middle of the empty loft. Inside it, spelled out in rose petals, was a message.

Do you believe in second chances?

"I do," Alec said, gesturing at the rose-petal message and answering her question. "I never got to say it that night but I love you. I have absolutely no idea how to raise a kid but my folks did a pretty good job with my siblings and me so we can call them for advice. And Bianca has a new baby so you'll be in good company… I just want a chance to do this together. That's what you're saying, right?"

"Yes. That's it. I love you, too, Alec. I've been so afraid to admit it because love and I aren't exactly on good terms so there might be times when I might panic and freak out but I want you to know I'm always coming back."

He could live with that. "I'm going to follow you."

He walked over to her and pulled her into his arms, kissing her with all the pent-up desire and emotion that had been building inside him for the last six weeks. "God, I missed you."

"I missed you, too," she said.

He patted his pocket and the ring box that he still had in there. He'd been carrying it around as if by doing so he'd bring Scarlet back to him. "I want to ask you to marry me, but there's no hurry. I know it's going to take time for you to feel safe living with me and our child, but know that's what I want."

"I'm going to say yes, but not today," she promised him. "I want to say yes when we both can believe that I mean it."

"I'll believe you," Alec told her. "You'd never make a promise you couldn't keep. Isn't that why you left?"

She nodded and then let her breath out in one long gasp. "Yes. I'll marry you!"

He carefully lifted her in his arms and hugged her as tightly as he could. "Thank you."

He took the ring box out of his pocket and put the ring on her finger. He'd picked out a princess-cut diamond and then had two smaller stones put on either side of it. He wanted to take her home and make love to her but it turned out his entire family was waiting outside Hadley's building when they exited.

"So, did you catch anything upstairs?" Mo asked.

"Just the love of my life," Alec responded.

Epilogue

One year later

Alec was sitting on the patio of the new home they'd had built just outside Cole's Hill, holding his tiny daughter, Tara Maria, in his arms while Scarlet lay next to him on the sun lounger. It was a gorgeous morning and the baby preferred to be outside so they spent most of their time outdoors.

Scarlet had decided to continue filming her reality TV show, and her fans were completely over the moon at the pregnancy and the baby. Alec was always monitoring their online footprint to ensure their privacy.

He had been careful so that he and the baby were only filmed in the periphery. She had successfully launched her wedding subscription box, along with one for expectant mothers, and was planning one for new moms later this year. He was proud of how hard she worked and that her public seemed to be accepting her new, more mature persona.

"So are you ever going to set a date for the wedding?" she asked him.

He glanced over at her. Since that day he'd asked her to marry him, he'd never brought it up again, knowing when she was ready she'd say the word. They'd been dividing their time between New York and Cole's Hill and probably would until Tara Maria was ready to start school.

"Are you ready?"

She nodded as the baby started to cry for her feeding. Scarlet breastfed her while he watched. His wife and his daughter. He'd never seen anything more beautiful and he'd never expected that having a family would enrich his life as much as it had.

"Then let's set a date. Kinley is dying to plan it," Alec said. "She pestered Nate into asking me about it last night at the Bull Pen."

They continued to discuss the details, and when Tara was fed and sleeping they took her into the nursery, which Scarlet had decorated in a soft floral theme.

Then he carried his soon-to-be wife to their adjoining bedroom and made love to her, knowing he'd achieved a happiness he'd never dreamed he'd find.

* * * * *

One by one,
the Velasquez men
are falling in love!

Find out
what's in store
for Inigo Velasquez
in

One Night to Risk It All

by USA TODAY *bestselling author*
Katherine Garbera.

Available December 2019
from Harlequin Desire.

COMING NEXT MONTH FROM

HARLEQUIN Desire

Available December 3, 2019

#2701 DUTY OR DESIRE

The Westmoreland Legacy • by Brenda Jackson

Becoming guardian of his young niece is tough for Westmoreland neighbor Pete Higgins. But Myra Hollister, the irresistible new nanny with a dangerous past, pushes him to the brink. Will desire for the nanny distract him from duty to his niece?

#2702 TEMPTING THE TEXAN

Texas Cattleman's Club: Inheritance • by Maureen Child

When a family tragedy calls rancher Kellan Blackwood home to Royal, Texas, he's reunited with the woman he left behind, Irina Romanov. Can the secrets that drove them apart in the first place bring them back together?

#2703 THE RIVAL

Dynasties: Mesa Falls • by Joanne Rock

Media mogul Devon Salazar is suspicious of the seductive new tour guide at Mesa Falls Ranch. Sure enough, Regina Flores wants to take him down after his father destroyed her family. But attraction to her target might take her down first...

#2704 RED CARPET REDEMPTION

The Stewart Heirs • by Yahrah St. John

Dane Stewart is a Hollywood heartthrob with a devilish reputation. When a sperm bank mishap reveals he has a secret child with the beautiful but guarded Iris Turner, their intense chemistry surprises them both. Can this made-for-the-movies romance last?

#2705 ONE NIGHT TO RISK IT ALL

One Night • by Katherine Garbera

After a night of passion, Inigo Velasquez learns that socialite Marielle Bisset is the woman who ruined his sister's marriage. A staged seduction to avenge his sister might quell his moral outrage... But will it quench his desire for Marielle?

#2706 TWIN SCANDALS

The Pearl House • by Fiona Brand

Seeking payback against the man who dumped her, Sophie Messena switches places with her twin on a business trip with billionaire Ben Sabin. When they are stranded by a storm, their attraction surges. But will past scandals threaten their chance at a future?

YOU CAN FIND MORE INFORMATION ON UPCOMING HARLEQUIN® TITLES, FREE EXCERPTS AND MORE AT WWW.HARLEQUIN.COM.

HDCNM1119

Get 4 FREE REWARDS!

We'll send you 2 FREE Books
plus 2 FREE Mystery Gifts.

Harlequin® Desire books feature heroes who have it all: wealth, status, incredible good looks... everything but the right woman.

FREE
Value Over
$20

A flash of pink moving around in his house made Kaegan frown when he
recalled just who'd worn that particular color tonight. He glanced back at
Sasha. "Tell Farley that I hope he starts feeling better. Good night." Without
waiting for Sasha's response, he quickly walked off, heading inside his
home.

He heard a noise coming from the kitchen. Moving quickly, he walked
in to find Bryce Witherspoon on a ladder putting something in one of the
cabinets. Anger, to a degree he hadn't felt in a long time, consumed him.
Standing there in his kitchen on that ladder was the one and only woman
he'd ever loved. The one woman he would risk his life for, and he recalled
doing so once. She was the only woman who'd had his heart from the time
they were in grade school. The only one he'd ever wanted to marry, have his
babies. The only one who...

He realized he'd been standing there recalling things he preferred not
remembering. What he should be remembering was that she was the woman
who'd broken his heart. "What the hell are you doing in here, Bryce?"

His loud, booming voice startled her. She jerked around, lost her balance
and came tumbling off the ladder. He rushed over and caught her in his arms
before she could hit the floor. His chest tightened and his nerves, and a few
other parts of his anatomy, kicked in the moment his hands and arms touched
the body he used to know as well as his own. A body he'd introduced to
passion. A body he'd—

"Put me down, Kaegan Chambray!"

He started to drop her, just for the hell of it. She was such a damn ingrate.
"Next time I'll just let you fall on your ass," he snapped, placing her on her
feet and trying not to notice how beautiful she was. Her eyes were a cross
of hazel and moss green, and were adorned by long eyelashes. She had high
cheekbones and shoulder-length curly brown hair. Her skin was a gorgeous
honey brown and her lips, although at the moment curved in a frown, had
always been one of her most noticeable traits.

"Let go of my hand, Kaegan!"

Her sharp tone made him realize he'd been standing there staring at her. He fought to regain his senses. "What are you doing, going through my cabinets?"

She rounded on him, tossing all that beautiful hair out of her face. "I was on that ladder putting your spices back in the cabinets."

He crossed his arms over his chest. "Why?"

"Because I was helping you tidy up after the party by putting things away."

She had to be kidding. "I don't need your help."

"Fine! I'll leave, then. You can take Vashti home."

Take Vashti home? What the hell was she talking about? He was about to ask when Vashti burst into the kitchen. "What in the world is going on? I heard the two of you yelling and screaming all the way in the bathroom."

Kaegan turned to Vashti. "What is she talking about, me taking you home? Where's Sawyer?"

"He got a call and had to leave. I asked Bryce to drop me off at home. I also asked her to assist me in helping you straighten up before we left."

"I don't need help."

Bryce rounded on him. "Why don't you tell her what you told me? Namely, that you don't need *my* help."

He had no problem doing that. Glancing back at Vashti, he said. "I don't need Bryce's help. Nor do I want it."

Bryce looked at Vashti. "I'm leaving. You either come with me now or he can take you home."

Vashti looked from one to the other and then threw up her hands in frustration. "I'm leaving with you, Bryce. I'll be out to the car in a minute."

When Bryce walked out of the kitchen, Kaegan turned to Vashti. "You had no right asking her to stay here after the party to do anything, Vashti. I don't want her here. The only reason I even invited her is because of you."

Kaegan had seen fire in Vashti's eyes before, but it had never been directed at him. Now it was. She crossed the room and he had a mind to take a step back, but he didn't. "I'm sick and tired of you acting like an ass where Bryce is concerned, Kaegan. When will you wake up and realize what you accused her of all those years ago is not true?"

He glared at her. "Oh? Is that what she told you? News flash—you weren't there, Vashti, and I know what I saw."

"Do you?"

"Yes. So, you can believe the lie she's telling you all you want, but I know what I saw that night."

Vashti drew in a deep breath. "Do you? Or do you only know what you think you saw?"

Then without saying anything else, she turned and walked out of the kitchen.

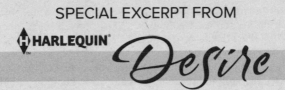
"That's it, Peterson Higgins, no more. You've had three servings already," Myra said, laughing, as she guarded the pan of peach cobbler on the counter.

He stood in front of her, grinning from ear to ear. "You should not have baked it so well. It was delicious."

"Thanks, but flattery won't get you any more peach cobbler tonight. You've had your limit."

He crossed his arms over his chest. "I could have you arrested, you know."

Crossing her arms over her own chest, she tilted her chin and couldn't stop grinning. "On what charge?"

The charge that immediately came to Pete's mind was that she was so darn beautiful. Irresistible. But he figured that was something he could not say.

She snapped her fingers in front of his face to reclaim his attention. "If you have to think that hard about a charge, then that means there isn't one."

"Oh, you'll be surprised what all I can do, Myra."

She tilted her head to the side as if to look at him better. "Do tell, Pete."

Her words—those three little words—made a full-blown attack on his senses. He drew in a shaky breath, then touched her chin. She blinked, as if startled by his touch. "How about 'do show,' Myra?"

Pete watched the way the lump formed in her throat and detected her shift in breathing. He could even hear the pounding of her heart. Damn, she smelled good, and she looked good, too. Always did.

"I'm not sure what 'do show' means," she said in a voice that was as shaky as his had been.

He tilted her chin up to gaze into her eyes, as well as to study the shape of her exquisite lips. "Then let me demonstrate, Ms. Hollister," he said, lowering his mouth to hers.

The moment he swept his tongue inside her mouth and tasted her, he was a goner. It took every ounce of strength he had to keep the kiss gentle when he wanted to devour her mouth with a hunger he felt all the way in his bones. A part of him wanted to take the kiss deeper, but then another part wanted to savor her taste. Honestly, either worked for him as long as she felt the passion between them.

He had wanted her from the moment he'd set eyes on her, but he'd fought the desire. He could no longer do that. He was a man known to forego his own needs and desires, but tonight he couldn't.

Whispering close to her ear, he said, "Peach cobbler isn't the only thing I could become addicted to, Myra."

Will their first kiss distract him from his duty?

Find out in
Duty or Desire
by New York Times *bestselling author Brenda Jackson.*

Available December 2019 wherever
Harlequin® Desire books and ebooks are sold.

Harlequin.com

Love Harlequin romance?

DISCOVER.

Be the first to find out about promotions,
news and exclusive content!

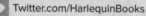 Facebook.com/HarlequinBooks

Twitter.com/HarlequinBooks

Instagram.com/HarlequinBooks

Pinterest.com/HarlequinBooks

ReaderService.com

EXPLORE.

Sign up for the Harlequin e-newsletter and
download a free book from any series at
TryHarlequin.com.

CONNECT.

Join our Harlequin community to share
your thoughts and connect with other
romance readers!
Facebook.com/groups/HarlequinConnection

 **HARLEQUIN®**

**ROMANCE WHEN
YOU NEED IT**

HSOCIAL2018